Hotel
Stories

Vincennes Writers Group

Presents:

Hotel

Stories

DEDICATION

To You, the reader.

CONTENTS

INTRO

Corridors. Hotels always have corridors.

Many people find these corridors haunting their dreams. Dreams about being chased, about hallways that go on and on with no end. Dreams where the doors close just before you reach them, slam, slam, slam. Halls where the doors on either side open onto to horrors unimagined. Or maybe that is just me.

But it is true that hotels and motels have long corridors. Long halls with lots of doors. Closed doors. Doors that hide lives behind them, lives that temporarily intersect when people emerge from the rooms behind the doors.

We hear whispers and laughter and shouts from behind the doors. We mingle with these others arbitrarily. We've stopped here for the night, they've stopped here for a week to hunt, or to go to Disneyland, or to attend the funeral of a family member. We see them in the elevator on our way out, we see them in the hotel pool, splashing water at their children. We brush against them in the common room where the continental breakfast is served, 6-8 a.m. every morning. Pour your own waffles. Butter your own toast. Listen to the visiting ball team chatter over orange juice about their chances against the home team. Itinerant lives sharing space, rubbing off on each other briefly, like the dust on a moth's wings.

Fate, chance, happenstance.

Some people crave the anonymous nature of hotels. Even the art is anonymous in nature; landscapes of indeterminate places, fuzzy and indistinct, or those splashy abstracts in tacky frames.

When I was younger, there were advertisements for "hotel/motel" art sales. Screaming announcers touting the bargains at the "Hotel /Motel Air Fair!" Where this art originated was never explained. Perhaps it came from the same factories that churned out the art that ended up in the rooms.

The rooms whose décor sported interchangeable color schemes of blue or orange or yellow or brown furnishings. Patterned bedspreads maximized to hide grime and wear. TVs bolted to the walls, and dark, heavy furniture with drawers containing nothing but a pen and pad, and a local phone book. The window, if the room has one, gives a view that doesn't vary from place to place. You see a field, a parking lot, a highway. Glimpses of the edges of cities that look exactly the same across the Midwest.

Back to our anonymous lodgings, safely tucked in for the night. Each room a tabula rosa in which, paradoxically, to make no mark. Housekeeping makes sure that you have no idea what went on in the room the day before.

This book is full of stories about some people who pass through those rooms, living their lives for a night or two behind the doors in the corridor. Sometimes those rooms are local to the States, and sometimes, shall we say, they are in another country.

Enjoy.

Jean
December 2014

LOST INN
B. T. Martinson

I can't believe I betrayed Samantha like that. Well, there are many things I can't believe. In the last 24 hours, I was at home with my fiancee, then at a training seminar, and, now, I'm staring out into a jungle while sipping coffee. I cannot believe who the woman sleeping in my bed is, either.

Yesterday, I hit the snooze button, and before I could rest my hand back on the bed, my fiancee, Samantha Higgins, whipped the covers off. I swear she found a way to do that while creating the greatest and coldest breeze possible.

"Ashton. Wake up," she cooed. I rolled over. Her blond hair brushed my shoulder. "Or our wedding will be hot pink and neon blue."

I pulled her close. "I think I'd look sexy in a neon blue tux and a hot pink tie."

"No argument there, but would your best man and groomsmen look as good?"

"I'll get the coffee started."

I reached for the alarm clock. I meant to turn the snooze off. When I tried, I knocked over a picture of Samantha and her little sister Maggie. Maggie was in a pale blue dress. I caught the photograph as soon as it fell, but there was a scraping sound as I corrected it. Samantha spun around at the noise. She gave me one of her annoyed looks, but, thankfully, she didn't say anything. Maggie died in a car accident when Maggie was seven and Samantha was nine. Samantha stares at that picture everyday, wishing things could be different. Not a day goes by where she wonders why it wasn't her that died.

I rolled out of bed and pulled up my to-do list on my phone. On the top of my priorities: wedding vows. The entire traditional contract that is marriage sums it up for me. I really didn't know how to elaborate on it.

I do believe my morning coffee makes everything better, but it does nothing to help me differentiate among the numerous bridal magazines Samantha hoards. I passed off her collection of bridal magazines as a quirk when we were dating, but I never imagined she planned to make me study them, too.

Samantha's blue eyes were dancing through a dozen possible weddings. "What flowers do you want for our wedding?"

I don't remember making any sounds when I looked over her shoulder, but I do remember thinking, how many times have I seen that exact same image in the past five days?

"Don't be such grouch. They're flowers. They're supposed to make people happy."

"I'm not a grouch. Most flowers look the same to me."

"I think we should go with the bouquet of lilies and roses. What colors?"

Apparently my stunned silence means I'm a jerk. She heaved an exasperated sigh. "Lilies and roses both come in a variety of colors. We can go blue and white, white and pink, pink and red..."

I should really have paid more attention in art class. I can understand code for programs, and I can wire anything. But, color combinations? They all look black and white to me.

"Um, the first one." Because I didn't really care about the flowers.

And, there's her hurt look. Again. "I thought it was a great idea."

She placed her hands on her hips, and asked, "What colors were the first one?"

I'll admit it. I am a jerk. "I meant the best ones."

She knows me pretty well. She told me I was trying to get out of it and take the easy way. Yup. She said, "I would like the colors to center around a light blue."

"Done! We'll have light blue everywhere."

Samantha's own blue eyes drilled into me. She knows exactly what looks kill me.

I went on. "Light blue is just as good for me as any other. Why does it matter?" She stared toward the picture. "Because light blue was Maggie's favorite color." She nodded.

"I think it's a great sentiment. Better than any testament that I could think of."

"That's not hard," she muttered.

"What's that supposed to mean?" I really was insulted. She doesn't pay any bills, I periodically surprise her with gifts, and I even cook dinner for her a few times a week. I don't understand what she wants.

"Testaments," she sighed. "Please tell me you're ready to start working on our vows."

Sometimes I hate my body. It involuntarily stepped back. After her jaw dropped from my reaction, I sputtered out, "I don't know how to elaborate on them. I think the ones spoken in every wedding ceremony I've ever been to sums it up for me."

"Because, I want to hear it from you."

"I've always been here," I replied.

"Here physically, but you never spend time with me. Instead of letting me get close to you, you always have a witty remark to change the subject. Or, you do something cute so you can slip away."

"That's a first... you must really hate Disney movies." I really need to filter my thoughts better. Before she could reply, I added, "I do want to spend the rest of my life with you. You're the reason I get out of bed every day. If not for you, I'd never get out of the house and try."

"You mean that?"

"Yeah, I know you do it with love when you whip the covers off of me."

She shook her head and crossed her arms. I put my hands on her shoulders. She did have the prettiest blue eyes, ever. I promised her, "I will work on my vows throughout the day. When I return, we will work on them together. It may be late, but I'll be back. I promise."

I was relieved to get away from her. I just needed time.

The seminar was terrible. It was two hours out of town, and in a cheap hotel. The presenter was intelligent. Actually, I'm assuming. The presenter was talking to the screen that he was working from most of the time. I think the only thing I heard him say was, "Does anyone have questions?" I didn't hear the rest of the presentation. From the material he was covering though, I'm guessing this guy was fresh out of college, and that the company he worked for thought they had made a major breakthrough. This seminar was a waste of time.

Exactly what I needed, or thought I needed. Everyone was scribbling notes about the presentation. I was scribbling notes about Samantha. The first vow I could think to make was working on being more open with her, and subduing my initial comments. After that, nothing. I wrote down the traditional wedding vows, all that I could think of, anyway. But, that didn't help either. I know Samantha wanted the wedding to be special. I'm just not sure how original I could make it. The more I thought about putting my feelings into vows, the more daunting the task seemed.

After the training seminar, I got something to eat at a diner, because I had a two hour drive home. Samantha called and left a message asking when I'd be home. I returned the call. I told her I would be home in a couple of hours, so around eight. I looked out the window of the diner and found that Mother Nature had decided she wanted to cover herself in a thick black blanket of clouds. I told Samantha it might be later if I don't beat the storm. I also told her I had some things to work on with the vows. I just didn't tell her that some things equaled one.

I stuffed the vows in my coat pocket, and I got on the highway as fast as I could. Then the storm promptly decided it was going to try opening the bowels of hell with sheer force of wind, rain, lightning, and thunder. The wind alone was enough to carry my car places I didn't want to go, and the rain only seemed to give the wind a substantial punch. Thunder normally doesn't bother me, but this storm had an omnipotent feel to it, where the thunder shook your bones.

In between gusts of rain, I spotted a rusted sign for The Lost Inn. The claw marks and bullet holes didn't show too well in the rain. It definitely wasn't a well kept sign.

Don't judge me. It was either this eerie looking hotel, or force my car to crawl home for the next 170 miles, after I had been cooped up in the basement of a cheap hotel with people I didn't care to get to know. So I took the exit into the forest.

The trees on either side of the road broke the raging wind, so at least there was that. About a quarter mile down the narrow road, I pulled up to a large inn. The storm had blocked out most of the daylight, so I missed a few details at first. The lightning wasn't willing to shine light on this place long enough for me to get a good look. I should have noticed that the entrance had bars that came down. It wasn't just the entrance. Every way into, or out of, the Inn had bars. No, this isn't a place that hoards supplies in case of a world disaster. On the contrary, that would be normal compared to this story.

Inside, the decor of the Inn was quaint. Most of it looked like it was homemade. Not that it was poorly built. In fact, it was extremely well built, but with poor taste. The fabric of the chairs was faded and stained. Each fabric was either a sickly green, or a tacky print with flowers. The cushions of the chairs and couch had lost their cushioning somehow. Think grandma's attic. Things go up there, but they never come back down. They go up there to be forgotten and die from neglect.

The walls of the lobby were adorned with some interesting paintings. I stopped at one. I thought it was a valley I had been to. The valley had beautiful sunsets, but this picture depicted what I thought was morning dew? It couldn't be. The sun doesn't rise from the west. The painting must be of a different valley.

I headed for the counter, where the clerk was cursing at his computer in a frustrated tone that grew higher with his blood pressure. Well, his version of cursing.

"Darn it, Sophia! Work, vex you. Work! Heavens, and Hades, and Earths, Work!" He slapped the computer and stomped off, his white coat flailing with his spastic movements. His white hair was a brillo-y tangle that bobbed with each angry step. "No, no, no. That's not it," he cried, and threw his arms out in front of him.

A woman's voice said, "The error occurred when-"

The man saw me and waved his arms in front of him in a sharp motion. He took a deep breath and carefully smoothed down his coat. His blues eyes caught the light in a way that made me look twice. I thought the light reflected in his eyes oddly, but the impression was gone before I could be sure.

I looked around for the source of light, but I couldn't discern where had come from. I thought it was my imagination.

"May I help you?"

"Who are you talking to?"

The man glanced at the computer. "I talk out loud when I'm frustrated." He took another steadying breath.

"I heard a woman's voice," I said.

He waved a hand toward the computer. "Er, computers."

It was my turn to take a steadying breath. "I need a room." I noticed there was a gun collection mounted up behind the counter. This was a state with a large number of hunters, so I didn't think much of it. I should've known better. If I ever get back home, I'll be sure to question everything.

"Will you be staying the night?" he asked. He kept blinking. When I looked closer, the odd light in his eyes was gone.

My next clue something was wrong. "Yeah."

"Oh, uh, well..." he drummed his fingers on the counter. He looked me up and down. "What do you do for a living?"

I took a breath. "I fix computers for a living. Most people and companies overwork their computers, pieces melt, pieces break, and machines get viruses. I can write programs, as well as build a computer from scratch if you need me to."

"Oh, excellent!" my host exclaimed. "Do you do wiring too?"

That's an odd question. "Sure. Can I help you?"

"Would you like to? I'll give you your room for free?"

Maybe I'm too fresh out of college, but the word free normally hooks me. "That's the best news I've heard all day."

"Great!" He exclaimed, and tapped his fist on the counter a few times as his smile dropped a little. "Do you have any family?"

"No, I was an only child."

"Are you married?"

"No." I didn't feel like telling him about Samantha. "What's with the questions?"

"Just small talk. That's all." He motioned for me to come around the counter. "The screen froze with the loading icon running. Nothing seems to work."

"What were you trying to do?"

"I was designing a... how should I phrase this? A device that can locate items in the quantum universes with teleport-like properties. I'm calling it the Q-Finder."

I was too surprised to be a smart ass, so I just stared. He said, "It's just a theory anyway. I was using a CAD program for the parts, when my computer froze. It seems to happen every few weeks now, and it takes me forever to find the problem."

"Sure." And, sure enough, there on the screen was a device with several satellite-looking cones projecting from a single hub with all the lights and whistles from a bad sci-fi show. "Um, when was the last time you saved your..." I wanted to say toy, but for a free room, I felt obligated to entertain the old man. "Q-Finder."

"Save?" Save as a question means no. "I-I don't know. I got so caught up in my work, you know?"

"Well, if there is a common room with coffee in it, how about I go get some coffee. And, while I'm gone, that will give you time to write down as much information from this locked screen as you can get. That way, you at least have the dimensions to go off of when you recreate it."

"Oh, wonderful! That's excellent news." At least, this guy was easy going and nice to be around. "There is a kitchen just down the hall, and it's the first door on your left."

"Thank you."

I remember feeling great about the Inn at this time. I checked my phone and thought about calling Samantha, but I felt like she hated me. I felt like she loved some idea in her head that she tried to project onto me. Every time I fell short of that idea, she condemned me a little more. Planning our wedding only seemed to exploit the differences between us, and if I dissented from her ideas, then I was the villain. I felt terrible about it.

Luckily, food loves me no matter what my opinions are.

Most hotels have a toaster, and a mini fridge with some drinks and bad bagels. I was pleasantly surprised to find a fully-equipped kitchen with a stainless steel refrigerator and a separate full freezer.

I found something that had coffee beans in it with a grinder button, so I made some fresh coffee after I figured out the weird design. Maybe the old had man designed it.

I explored the stainless steel cabinets and found more appliances and food.

"Looking for something?" a man's voice inquired.

I turned and found a guy behind me dressed in all white, with a black apron that barely fit around his large frame and belly. "I was, uh, looking for coffee mugs."

"Of course. One cabinet to your left."

"Thanks." I carefully opened the cabinet to retrieve a mug.

"Can I fix you anything to eat?"

"I wasn't planning on it. I don't have much money on me. Do you take credit cards?"

"Um, yes. I take credit." I couldn't quite place his accent. It sounded French, but it was off a little bit. Almost like it had a bit of Scandinavian mixed in with it.

"Great, what do you have to eat?"

"What do you like to eat?"

I said, "Well, I guess I normally chicken out and take the safe route with the chicken."

He smiled. "Yes, and do you want, uh, what do you call them, plants?"

"Vegetables? Sure. English isn't your native language."

He ran a hand over a day's worth of black stubble on his olive colored chin. "No. It is not. I am from very far from here."

"Where are you from?"

"Jestulvous. It is a small that place that many people have not heard of unless they are from there. I will cook your chicken and vegetables. You wait in dining room."

I told him thanks, and followed his gesture, going out the swinging doors and into a ballroom. A ballroom in an inn. I knew this place was big, but this was insane. Tables lined what would be a dance floor. A magnificent chandelier hung over the center. And, in the center of the dance floor was a woman with an easel. Her blue eyes stared intently at the painting while she brushed in shadows.

I approached the blond bombshell. She wore baggy clothes, but the apron she wore revealed a small waist, and hinted at a nice bust.

"If you need a model, I'll gladly apply."

She snapped her blue eyes on me, and I faltered. That face was quite similar to Samantha's.

To my surprise, she smiled at my lame approach. "Not at the moment." She looked me up and down. "Maybe later, though. Are you staying?"

"For a night."

She looked at her watch. "It's never too late to change your mind. I'm sure Dewey would understand."

"It's just a night."

"Won't a wife, or fianceé be concerned about you?"

"Samantha will be alright for one night. She needs time to think about the wedding." The painter smiled at the mention of Samantha.

"I'm sure she will miss you if you stay."

"The storm is terrible."

"All storms come to an end?"

"A philosopher and a painter, huh?" I remarked. She smirked. Wow. Even when her face was covered in paint, that smile was mesmerizing.

She brushed a blond lock of hair out of her face with

the back of a hand. "I have to talk to Dewey. I hope you find your way home," she said, and ran off. She checked her watch one last time before she went through the door.

I looked at my own watch. I should get back to the receptionist soon. I had told him I would help get his computer working again.

I glanced at her painting. The scene was of this ballroom, but filled with musicians, dancers, and entertainers. It looked like a great party. In the center of it was a woman that looked like the artist, and she wore a beautiful, light blue dress. I wondered idly if that was what Samantha's wedding dress might look like. I entertained the idea of them throwing a party like that in here. Why else would they have a place like this?

I'm not sure how long I stared at the painting, but I was still staring at it when the cook brought out my meal. "She has much talent. She paints them from memory."

"Oh, yeah, she's great. And she does this from memory?" The cook nodded. I entertained the idea of why she had looked me up and down, and smiled.

"Your dinner is ready." He motioned toward a table with a plate holding a mound of chicken and vegetables on it. "What would you like to drink? We have wines and whiskeys of excellent years. We also have water, coffee, and juices of all kinds."

"I'll take a white wine. One that'll complement the chicken nicely."

"I know the very one."

He had fixed two giant chicken breasts with Italian-like spices, and zesty juices. I took a bite. Heavenly. He came back with the wine. "This is amazing. What's in it?"

He winked at me. "That is my secret." He set a wine glass on the table and opened the wine. I didn't recognize the name, but I did notice the year. It was from 1814. This had to be impossible.

"Shouldn't that be vinegar?"

He shook his head no. "Some wines, yes. But, this one, no. Depends on the wine. This should last another century before it turns to vinegar."

"Please, sit. Tell me about yourself." If this guy was giving me a 200 year old wine without a second thought, I could give him some of my time. When I look back, if I had turned this drink down, maybe I would have been thinking clearly enough to jump ship and head back home in time. "What's your name?"

"You may call me Edgar Blanc. I cook for the Inn. I have been a resident here for 20 years. I started when I was fifteen." He looked good for his age. "I enjoy cooking very much. I am always trying new recipes. What do you do?"

"I work on computers."

"Very interesting. What, uh, kind of computers?"

"I don't care if it's a Mac or PC. If it's broken I can fix it. Doesn't matter if it's the hardware or the software. I know both, inside and out."

"Good. This has treated you well, and you enjoy it very much?"

"Yes, I do enjoy it." I didn't want to tell him that the job was getting routine. Yes, computers double their advances in a few short years, but once you know the basics, and how the technology advances, you pretty much know what to expect.

"Your friends and family must be proud of you?"

"Computers are my friends. I feel like I know them better than my own fiancee."

"You and your fiancee; you fight?"

I nodded. "Have you ever been married?" Edgar shook his head. "I thought I knew her so well. Then the pieces just stopped fitting together. I don't know why I keep trying to make them fit."

"I am sorry to hear that," he said. "Maybe what you need is a good adventure? Yes?"

I scoffed at the comment.

"Maybe you should sleep on it, then. The world is a very strange place."

"Right now, it seems pretty grand to me." Ironic. I know. Edgar checked his watch. "I should be going."

Before he could push himself from the table, the blond came back in with the clerk in tow looking like a puppy that had just been caught peeing on the carpet.

The artist stepped out and said, "Dewey has something to tell you."

Edgar's chair grunted when he pushed it out, and her blue eyes drilled him into submission. "Did you tell him?"

Edgar shrugged. "How do you tell someone?"

"Boys." She threw Dewey in front of me. "Tell him, Dewey. He hasn't got much time."

Only now did I start to get worried. And, little did I know, it was way too late.

Dewey ringed his hands, "Well, uh, I am working on this. It's why I need you to fix my computer, and why I need to build the Q-Finder. So, I can control all of this." I gave him my best deer in headlights look. It wasn't difficult. "You see, this Inn got its name from its nature. My family built it. And, well, it has a tendency to wander."

"Wander? As in it grows legs, and walks off?"

He laughed. "No, that would be simple. The atoms comprising it become unstable and slip into another universe. Which one, I have no idea. If I could build the Q-Finder, I might be able to control where it goes."

The disembodied voice of the woman sounded again from Dewey. "The Lost Inn travels between parallel universes due to an anomaly in a teleportation device. The Inn itself was teleported. The machine keeps the atoms stable for 24 hours at a time before it has to reassemble them. The reassembly occurs in universes at random."

I looked around, and the group stared at me while I searched for the source of the voice. When it stopped, I asked, "Who and what was that?"

Dewey cleared his throat. "That was Sophia. My AI that aids me in my work." He held up an odd watch that didn't tell time. "She's built into my coat, so she follows me everywhere. However, she enjoys using the speaker when she wants to talk to other people."

I gave a nervous laugh. "I think I may have had too much wine. What on Earth are you talking about?"

Sophia hummed. "He doesn't understand."

Edgar spoke up, "Jestulvous isn't on this Earth. It's on a different Earth. One that doesn't exist here, but very much does in another universe."

"What?"

Dewey ran a hand over his bald head and into the ring of white hair. "The Inn's atoms become unstable after 24 hours. Every night at midnight, the atoms, in a sense, fall apart and reassemble themselves, but in a parallel universe."

"They fall apart? Everything?" He nodded. "And, everyone." He nodded again.

I checked my watch. 11:45pm. I still had 15 minutes to walk out the door. I'm fine. "In that case," I said. "I think I should get going."

"We understand," Blondie said. "We'll walk you out."

My phone rang on queue. Samantha. "Hi, honey." I continued for the exit as I talked.

"Where are you?"

"I've stopped at an inn because of the storm. I'm heading home now."

"When did you plan on telling me this?" she asked.

"When you've cooled down," I replied.

"You're such a child."

"I'm on my way home now. I'll see you soon."

"Don't bother."

"What?" I stopped at the ballroom doors. Edgar and Dewey stood with one foot and ear towards me while their eyes pointedly looked everywhere else. Blondie glared at them.

"You would rather spend your time on anything else than me."

Blondie gave me a push. I headed out.

"Samantha. I'd do anything for you."

"To buy me off. I don't want things, and I can take care of myself."

If Blondie hadn't been pushing me, I would've stopped. I was nearly jogging to stay ahead of her.

"That's not true. It doesn't mean I don't love you."

I opened the door and the rain roared a dare at me.

"Do you really love me?" Samantha asked. I could barely hear her over the rain.

I saw the world pulse and waver. It's amazing how fast your priorities change when your life is on the line, or a moment of complete paradigm shift is in front of you. "Samantha. I love you."

"Prove it."

I ran as hard as the rain fell. I reached my car and fumbled for my keys. Then the world pulsed again and stopped. Then it fell apart into nothing. 'Nothing' is an odd experience. Feelings and thoughts cease. The feeling of clothes against your skin, gravity holding you to the earth, smells, sounds, and even the feeling of your own blood coursing through your veins completely stops. It's unnerving, really. I watched my body fall apart. Then, a second later, the world fell together again. Even the rain. The rain that was caught in the vicinity of the Inn fell to the ground and then came to an abrupt halt. I looked up at the stars. Stars that shone past the roof of a jungle.

"I am so sorry," Blondie said.

I raised the phone to my ear. "Samantha?"

Dial tone. I called her again. Dial tone. "Samantha?"

Sophia hummed and lamented, "This Earth is a primitive one with no remote access to a collective intelligence or network. Samantha cannot hear you from here."

"Does she always do that?" I seethed.

Dewey placed a hand on my shoulder. "I should have told you."

"We'll come back with time," Blondie suggested.

"How long?" I asked.

Dewey shook his head. "No way to tell."

Sophia hummed, "With an unknown number of parallel universes and random chances it may take up to 2,568 Earth years-"

"Not now, Sophia," I barked and looked at the little group. They all took a step back from me. I took a deep breath. "This Q-Finder. Can it find my home?"

Dewey nodded.

"I need to fix your computer."

"Can I get you anything?" Blondie asked.

"More wine?" I asked, and she nodded.

"Thanks, Blondie."

"Maggie Higgins," she quipped. "Pleased to meet you."

"Higgins? Do... did you have any family?"

"I had a sister, Samantha, but she died in a car accident when I was seven. I sometimes wonder if she's alive in one of the other universes."

"Better make it whiskey," I said. "I can't believe this."

Maggie placed a hand on my shoulder and tried to console me. I don't remember much after that. I was just hoping that if I fell asleep, I would wake up in my own bed, with a funny dream to tell people. But, no, I really am in a different parallel universe now. On a different Earth. I woke up in a bed that belonged in a grandma's attic. Worse, Maggie is still in my bed. I don't even remember what we did last night.

Only thing I can do now is help Dewey make his Q-Finder, in the hope that he can find a way back to my universe. I hate the name of this place. The Lost Inn. That might be the understatement of all of the universes.

NEGOTIATIONS AT HELL'S
BED & BREAKFAST
N. E. Riggs

"Welcome to our Bed and Breakfast, beautiful. It's only a quaint place, I know, but I hope you enjoy your stay." The speaker leaned across the desk, his talons drawing lazy circles. A long tongue hung out his mouth, pointed at the end.

Lailah held her sword and suitcase tight. The walls of the reception area were made of bones. Blood dripped off of them and pooled on the floor. Red splashed whenever she took a step. A creature that might have once been human shuffled forward, its knees tied together. It tried to take her suitcase, but Lailah didn't let go.

She couldn't look away from the monster behind the desk. He had sharp teeth now, and horns protruded through thick, dark curls. The talons and pointed tongue were new, too. Still, she knew him. "Gressil?"

His smile widened. "You do remember me. How marvelous. Do you remember the times we sang together, practiced fighting together? The times we held one another so close? I do."

"That was a long time ago, and we are both much changed. My room key?" She stuffed her suitcase under her arm and held out a hand. She didn't release her sword – not in a place like this.

"I hadn't heard you'd be the one coming to negotiate." A rack of keys hung behind Gressil – he made no move to take any down. "Rights over Las Vegas, isn't it?"

"Yes."

Gressil tsked. "That you lot think you have any chance of taking that city from our possession. What gall! Is there anywhere on Earth where more people go to hope than Las Vegas – only to have all their hope taken from them?"

Lailah shook her open hand at Gressil. "My trip was long and tiring, and very unpleasant. I would like to retire to my room."

"What, and miss catching up? So impolite! That isn't like your kind." Gressil's smile grew. "But then, you've never been like the others of your kind, have you, angel of the night?"

A growl and a hiss came from behind her, followed by a splash of something moving over blood-soaked carpets. Lailah whirled, her sword swinging without her having to think. She batted the imp aside a moment before its claws could reach her. Its small, hard body hit the ground with a thud.

The second imp had hidden in the shadow of the first, and Lailah almost missed it. It had to shift to avoid the first imp as it rolled. Lailah jumped to the side, and her suitcase dropped. Her sword cut through the air, fast as lightning, and separated the imp's head from its body.

Something sharp dragged at her leg. Lailah kicked out, connecting with the imp she'd batted aside moments ago. She shifted, wincing as she put weight on her leg. She ignored the pain and plunged her fiery sword into the imp's chest. It went still.

Lailah heard something else from behind her, and whipped around, her sword moving faster than her eyes. With a sharp clang, it stopped. Gressil stood, a naked blade in his hands, easily holding her back. His smile had lost none of its size.

"I'm so sorry. The bellhops can be impertinent."

Lailah bared her teeth as she stepped away from Gressil. He didn't follow her up, lowering his sword first. She shifted to favor her right foot. The first imp had cut her, she could tell without looking. Hopefully, not too deep. She'd expected many attacks on this trip, but none so soon. "So long as they weren't expecting a tip."

Gressil threw his head back and laughed. He tossed his sword aside – it landed neatly on a rack behind the desk. "I see that floating in the clouds and singing praises to God haven't dulled your tongue entirely. Good."

Without looking away from Gressil, Lailah bent and picked up her suitcase. "I am an ambassador here, invited by your kind." She couldn't keep the scorn out of her voice, didn't really try. "Did you really think attacking me would be wise? Or that I'd be defeated so easily? Such foul creatures would never kill me!" She kicked the headless imp in its side.

"No one with sense thought that. Sadly, the imps are not that clever." Gressil shook his head. He finally took a key from the rack and motioned for Lailah to follow him. "I'm sure all the negotiations will be in good faith."

"I'm sure," Lailah echoed, the sarcasm dripping heavier than the blood.

Gressil led her from the reception area to a hallway. Bones of countless damned humans made up the place. The blood seemed heavier here, and it was very dark. That didn't bother Lailah. She needed no light to see. The night was her time.

"Here." Gressil unlocked the fourth door and held it open, sweeping a majestic bow and motioning her inside. "Lovely, comfortable beds, perfect for an orgy or two. Two hundred channels, including the best zoophilia, necrophilia, and coprophilia, no extra charge."

"I brought a book," Lailah said.

"I'm sure you did. Always so restrained. Never letting

yourself do what you want to do." She felt a hand on the back of her neck, talons feathering over her.

She whirled and tried to get her sword up, but Gressil was too close. The angle was no good. He grinned wider and pushed her. Her back pressed against a wall of bones. Gressil held her in place, his strength far greater than hers. Even still, she could have attacked him, could have sliced into him. She didn't.

"And what," she said slowly, "do you know about what I want?" Gressil didn't strangle her, only held her neck tight. She was keenly aware of how easily his grip could grow stronger, how he could smother her against the wall. If she had attacked sooner, she might have stopped him before this. Her heart beat wildly, and not in fear.

"I know you, Lailah." He spoke into her ear, his breath hot and smelling of sulfur. "We were once inseparable, you and I. I miss you. I miss those days. Don't you?"

She glared. "You were the one who left. Not me."

"And why shouldn't I?" He pulled back so Lailah could see him. Maybe it was the light, maybe it was how close he stood to her. But the horns and talons and sharp teeth that had made him so repulsive in the reception area now seemed to fit him. He had chosen them, made them part of him. His smile said he knew that, and liked it. "I'm happy here, Lailah. I'm free, to do whatever I wish."

"And you think I'd be happier, too, here?"

Gressil nodded. One talon caressed her neck, running shivers down her spine – not the unpleasant kind. Even his closeness to her now felt intimate rather than threatening. "The night is yours, and everything that comes with it. Lies, violence, suspicion. Sex." He whispered the last word into her ear. "Those things are part of you, too, Lailah. Why fight it?"

Lailah shook her head as much as she could. "You make the same mistake everyone does. There is nothing evil in the night – not inherently. The only evil that lives in the darkness is what we bring – same as the day."

"Perhaps. But you desire me." Gressil molded himself to her, connecting their bodies at every point. She no longer held her sword, she realized, as he entwined his fingers with hers. "We held the night together once. We can do it again. I want you, more than anything. We belong together. Don't you want that?"

"Of course." The words slipped out before she could stop them. Lailah went stiff and pressed her lips together.

Gressil smiled and pulled away from her. "I thought so. Enjoy your stay, my sweet. You know where to find me when the night grows long and your book proves insufficient entertainment." He slipped out the door before Lailah could say anything else.

With shaking hands, she pulled her suitcase and sword off the floor, trying to ignore the blood that dripped from them. "He would leave at that." Gressil always knew when and how to time himself. He could have pushed. Now she was alone, and could only wonder what it would have felt like if Gressil hadn't left.

Their encounter weighed on her mind throughout her stay in Hell. She tried to pay attention during negotiations, couldn't. The harder she tried to focus on the lost souls of Las Vegas, the more she could feel Gressil's hand on her neck, Gressil's breath in her ear, Gressil's body flush against her own.

The negotiations went badly. Her arguments fell on deaf ears. The demons ignored her best arguments – they'd never wanted this discussion anyway. They repeated that Las Vegas was theirs and always would be. Eventually, they agreed to extra Gambler's Anonymous groups, and more homeless shelters. A pathetic concession, far less than Lailah had hoped. She tried to console herself, told herself that this was the best she ever could have expected. Las Vegas has long been in the grip of evil.

With bitterness, she packed her suitcase and left. Her

feet dragged as she walked down the hallway, and every time she stepped, blood splashed up, splattering her white robes. She wanted to scream. She wished more imps would attack her, so she could work out some of her frustration. She saw nothing move in the hallway.

At the reception area, Gressil leaned against his desk. Lailah's breath caught. She hadn't seen him since she arrived, but he had never been far from her thoughts. She cursed herself as she took in his appearance.

"I'm sorry your meetings went so poorly." Gressil didn't smile, looked genuinely distressed. He had always played games so easily, Lailah reminded herself, even long ago, when there had been no cruelty to his games. "I wish I could do something to help." He stepped closer to her.

Lailah had her sword sheathed, and made no move to draw it. "Do you miss me?"

His hand caught a strand of her hair, twisted it between his fingers. "Every minute of every day. I'm happier than ever, Lailah, but how can I be completely happy without you? We were created to be together."

"I know. I miss you, too. I didn't realize how much – I wouldn't let myself realize how much." She leaned closer to him, pressing her cheek against his shoulder. If she closed her eyes, she could imagine him as the person he'd been so long ago. If she let herself go, she could imagine him as he currently was – and that he was still lovely.

Hands rested on her waist, loose and easy to escape if she wanted to. She didn't. "Stay with me. Promise to be with me forever, and I'll do anything you want."

She closed her eyes. The lost negotiations faded from her memory as if they'd never happened. "Gressil, I do love you. I want to be with you, no matter what."

"So do I. Promise me, Lailah. Please. I need you."

"I promise." Dropping her suitcase, she caught his face between her hands. She saw no darkness around him now. There was only Gressil. "I will be with you forever."

Gressil tipped his head back, his smile stretched impossibly wide. "Oh, Lailah, you don't know how happy you've made me. You won't regret your choice. I swear I won't let you down."

"I know. Which is why you'll come back to heaven with me." Gressil stared, his mouth hanging open. "You owe me, Gressil. Anything I want. I'm going back home, and we're going to be together forever. So you'd better come with me." She released his face and grabbed his hand. She dragged him from the hotel, from Hell.

He followed her, clutching her hand tight. At first his talons bit into her hand, but only at first. His talons faded away the higher Lailah and Gressil rose, until they disappeared altogether. "How?" he whispered as they reached the gates of heaven. "How can you do this, Lailah?"

She laughed. "I am the angel of the night, and everything that entails. Love together is strongest in the dark. We shared it before, and we will again. You can't resist me." And when she pulled him past the gates, he never looked back.

N E Riggs

NIGHT WIND
Molly Daniels

"Thank you for staying with us, and come back again."
Jennifer handed the elderly couple their receipt and smiled.
"Be careful going home."

"Thank you, dear. We will." The woman patted the top
of the honey-oak reception desk and turned, taking her
husband's arm. He led her across the dark blue carpeted
floor to the automatic doors.

A sudden scream disrupted the tranquil morning.
"Stop him! Somebody help!"

Jeni shoved the small swinging door to her left,
grimacing when it ricocheted off the wall and smacked her
left hip. She grasped the gleaming brass rail of the staircase
and reeled backward as a young man in a short red bellhop
coat sent her crashing against the oak paneling. Before she
could recover, a second body barreled down the stairs,
missed the final two steps, and sprawled on the marble floor.
Jeni regained her balance and helped the man struggle to his
feet.

"Stop that man!" He brushed Jeni aside as a valet
parking attendant grabbed the bellhop in his beefy arms
and slammed him to the blue floor mat. The man Jeni had
helped ran over to the attendant and rummaged through

the bellhop's pocket. With a triumphant 'Ah-ha!' as he held up a gold watch. "Call the police. How dare you try to steal someone else's belongings!" He slapped the thief's face.

Jeni glanced toward the reception desk, where her manager, Lee Chauncey, ended a call and hurried over. "Jeni, please move the onlookers to the sitting area. Anyone who witnessed this, the police will want to speak to them." To the perspiring gentleman, he raised his hands, palms outward. "The police are on their way. Thank you for your quick actions, AJ."

Aaron 'AJ' Jeffries struggled to his feet, still gripping the angry bellhop, who twisted and tried to break loose. "All in a day's work, boss. Just doing my job." He face-planted the young man into the wall and yanked his arms behind him. "Where's Hugh?"

Tugging her blue uniform shirt back into place, Jeni stepped toward the gathering onlookers. She repeated Lee's instructions, and tried to answer questions as best as she could.

Hugh, their security guard and retired policeman, strode into the lobby, brushing the crumbs from his black jacket. "I'm sorry boss. I was called away to break up a food fight. Teenagers." He produced his handcuffs and secured the thief to a brass railing. "What's going on?"

Lee brought him up to date as the wailing sound of sirens filled the air. Soon, a pair of uniformed policemen entered the building. One took the man into custody, while the other stayed behind to interview those in the lobby.

Lee and Jeni answered the officer's questions, then Lee retrieved the security video, while Jeni returned to her post at the reception desk. Jeni fielded an onslaught of phone calls, and apologized for the delays in checkout. Guests who hadn't seen anything were cleared to check out of the Worthington Arms Hotel and return to their lives. Those who had witnessed the attack were a mixture of agitated and calm regarding the sudden change in schedule. The agitated ones were the most vocal.

"I'm going to miss my plane." A harried-looking woman pulled out her iPhone and typed furiously.

A businessman in his early forties, his face red with anger, demanded, "Now see here, if I don't make my meeting, I'll lose a potential billion dollar sale." The officer took him aside, and after a quiet conference, let him go.

"Any of you with flights to catch, or something that absolutely cannot wait, see me," Jeni heard the officer say. A group quickly formed around him.

The man who had chased the thief finished giving his statement, then approached the front desk. "Will you please contact Mr. Kross and let him know his property has been recovered?" He mopped his flushed face with a white handkerchief.

"I've already spoken to Mr. Malone. He called down earlier, and I've reassured him nothing like this has ever happened before. Has Mr. Kross ordered breakfast yet?" Lee looked at Jeni. "I'll handle things down here. Please go with Mr-"

"Parsons. Greg Parsons, Aiden Kross's manager." He shook Jeni's hand. "Thank you for helping me up. No, we have not ordered breakfast yet."

Jeni handed him a menu. "Order what you want, compliments of the house." She phoned the restaurant and spoke to the hostess, who took his order. Jeni accompanied Greg back upstairs, her stomach in knots. She'd been a fan of Aiden Kross for years, even before he'd topped the music charts. Since she worked the day shift, she had been thrilled when Lee had taken her aside and told her of their famous guest. As she and Greg rode the elevator to the private suite, she reminded herself to be professional.

Greg paused outside the suite. "Mr. Kross values his privacy. I've no doubt he'll want to speak to you in person, but please don't be one of those obnoxious people who want him to sign everything."

Jeni smiled and nodded. *Does he think I'm an idiot? I do know how to be professional.*

Greg knocked on the door, a series of knocks meant to be code. "I left without my key."

"Not to worry." Jeni pulled out her key ring. "I have a master key." She inserted it into the lock at the same time the door opened. For the second time in an hour, Jeni found herself falling, this time head first into a set of rock-hard abs. She went to her knees, taking down a potted plant, and grabbed at the denim-clad legs to stop her fall. The man grunted and flailed as he lost his balance, grabbing her dark hair in the process. Jeni let go of his knees as she rolled onto her back, thankful for the thick carpeting. Panting and holding onto her side where she'd collided with the plant, Jeni looked up into the startled eyes of Greg Parsons.

"Jesus, Mary, and Joseph," wheezed the man she'd knocked down. Jeni turned her head and saw the half-dressed man push himself from the back of the sitting area couch. "Greg, I heard your signal, man. What gives?"

"Sorry, Sam. She had her key out before I could say anything." Greg helped Jeni to her feet. "Sam, this is Jeni, assistant manager. Sam Malone, Aiden's bass player."

"Sam Malone? As in-" Jeni shut her mouth.

"Yeah, yeah, same as Ted Danson's character in Cheers. My parents have a sense of humor." Sam grimaced, then shook her hand. "How did you know that name? That show went off the air in the mid nineties."

Jeni smiled. "My parents recently began watching it on NetFlix on my account. I've caught a few episodes."

"Unbelievable." Sam cleared his throat. "Greg, Aiden's taking a shower."

"Shit. He needs to sleep more." Greg closed the door after pulling Jeni's key ring from the lock. "Why doesn't this hotel have those key cards? I told you we should have stayed somewhere else."

"Tell Aiden that." Sam pointed his thumb at the closed door. "He said the fans would look for him at a newer hotel, and he had a soft spot in his heart for this place."

"He's stayed here before?" Jeni blurted, then felt her face burn with embarrassment.

The inner door opened and Aiden Kross, current media and music world darling, entered, clad in only a white monogrammed bathrobe. Curly brown chest hair protruded from the deep vee of the collar. Jeni felt her knees go weak. *Do not go all fangirl on him!*

"What's with all the racket?" He yawned and stretched his arms above his head. The knee-length robe showed tanned, muscular legs. He dropped his arms to his side, a ten-kilowatt smile lighting up his face. "Hi, darlin'. What can I do for you?"

Oh my God. He smiled at me.

Shut up. That's his standard line.

Jeni fixed a smile on her face. "Mr. Kross, I'm the assistant manager, here to assure you we have everything under control." She felt a hand brush her hair and jerked her head to the side to see Greg toss a leaf on the floor.

Aiden walked toward the sink in the kitchenette. "Everything under control, eh? Then why is my manager plucking leaves from your hair, Greg chasing people from the room, and Sam telling me police are downstairs?" Without waiting for an answer, he turned on the tap and filled a glass full of water.

"Mr. Kross-"

"Call me Aiden. Mr. Kross is my father." He downed the liquid. "Ahhh...that's what I always liked about this place. The water's so clean and fresh-tasting. Better than that bottled stuff."

Jeni moved closer. "Greg ordered breakfast, and it's on the house, Mr-er, Aiden. The unfortunate person has been taken into custody, and I can assure you the rest of your stay should be stress free."

Aiden snorted. "Stress free, she says. Only until the media gets wind of where I'm actually staying." He took another glass from the cabinet and filled it.

Jeni felt her face burn again.

"Relax, darlin'." Aiden handed her the second glass. "I go through this everywhere I go. Someone always leaks my actual location. We're doing one show tonight at the university, so we'll be out of your hair around six tonight. Hopefully the bus's transmission will be fixed by then and we can be back on the road after the show."

"Won't you want to unwind here after the show, instead of leaving right away?" Jeni gasped. "I would think this would be more comfortable than the bus."

The men laughed. Aiden shook his head, his brown curls brushing his cheek. "Settle down; clearly we have someone who doesn't understand rock stars. My travel trailer is way more comfortable than someone else's bed. The only downfall is finding food without being recognized. Here, I'm trapped, unless I manage to sneak out incognito, but that's not always the case." He took another swallow of water. "It's okay, Jen. I appreciate all you've done for us."

A knock sounded at the door along with "Room service!"

Jeni hurried to it and looked through the peephole, recognized the head server, Sharon, and opened the door. The other woman wheeled the cart inside and pointed out the items on the tray before respectfully leaving the room. Greg lifted the white tablecloth covering the bottom and, satisfied fans hadn't tried to sneak in, turned to Jeni.

"Thank you for everything."

"You're welcome. If there's anything else you need, please don't hesitate to call the front desk." Jeni turned the knob but halted when Aiden's voice stopped her.

"Here, give this to the pretty waitress for her trouble." Aiden nodded at Greg, who pulled some bills from his wallet. "And it goes without saying, you don't tell anyone you've been up here."

Jeni's spine stiffened. "Your location is safe with me, Mr. Kross. Break a leg tonight, don't worry about the night wind, and bang a drum for me." She couldn't help mentioning the lyrics to her favorite song as she exited the room.

* * *

"Well I'll be damned." Greg shook his head as he fastened the security chain. "She's a cool one. Never let on she was a fan."

Aiden stroked his chin. "That was one of my earlier hits. She must have seen me when I was playing the small bars. It's not on any platinum album."

"Maybe she got it off YouTube?" Sam sat down at his laptop.

"Even if she did, why did her voice go all stiff and cold?" Aiden placed both glasses in the sink. "No, she's pissed about something. Maybe because I reminded her-damn it, she's management. She'd never break a confidence. Why'd I have to say that? I insulted her." He slapped the counter. "It is too damn early to be handling all this drama. Let's eat." Aiden strode to the sitting area while Greg rolled the cart to the center of the couch, loveseat, and chair arrangement. He piled his plate high with bacon, eggs, and hash browns, then took a seat on the sofa.

After they'd eaten, Aiden rubbed his full stomach, then picked up the phone and dialed the front desk. "Jen? Hi, it's Aiden. Look, I didn't mean to insult you earlier.....yeah....look, would you be interesting in coming to the concert tonight? You quoted one of my....yeah. Seriously? Where did you hear them?" He sat up. "No way. You've got to be shitting me....yeah, I'll leave you a ticket at Will Call. Bring that photo, will you? Thanks, darlin'....see you later tonight." Aiden hung up and shook his head. "No fucking way. Greg, do you remember ten years back, when we found this place?"

Greg chewed, and took a swig of coffee. "Yeah. Did she work here or something?"

"No." Aiden placed his plate on the coffee table and stood up to pace. "We were just starting out, and were traveling around in that piece of shit Jeep you owned-"

"Hey, that Jeep got us where we are today." Greg mumbled around a mouthful of eggs, then coughed. Sam slapped him on the back.

"The Jeep blew a tire outside of town, and that man stopped and gave us a ride to town. We didn't have any money to pay the mechanic, so I whipped out my guitar and did an impromptu concert in the park next door--"

Greg jumped up. "School had just let out and all those kids came running over to hear the music. I found a box and passed it around for donations, then you posed for pictures and sold a few CDs. Don't tell me she was one of 'em."

Aiden grinned. "Yup. She's got the picture I took with her and her friend, and one of my original discs. I knew coming back here for that concert was a good decision."

Sam whistled. "Un-be-lievable. So, you inviting her backstage?"

"Yup." Aiden stroked his chin in a thoughtful manner. "If I remember correctly, she's the one who urged everyone to empty their pockets and help pay the tow bill. She's still got the IOU I signed, indicating next time I came here, I'd show her a good time."

Greg choked. "If she was in high school then, she'd be mid-twenties, Aiden. What kind of a 'good time' do you plan to show her?"

"Grow up." Aiden scowled at his manager. "I've grown out of the sleep-with-every-groupie-I-can phase. I'll give her a great seat, show her around backstage, and since she knows Night Wind, invite her to sing it with me. If she can sing, that is. Greg, I'll need you to get her to sing a few lines before you bring her backstage just before the encore."

"What the hell are you going to do if she can't sing?" Greg refreshed his coffee.

"Then I'll sing it to her. Make a note and have a stool ready, in case she's tone-deaf." Aiden strode into the bedroom and closed the door.

* * *

Later that evening

Jeni's fingers shook as she slipped into denim Capri pants and a yellow sleeveless Polo shirt. Shoving her feet into plain white tennis shoes, she plucked the creased picture from the frame of her dresser mirror. She smoothed the faces of herself, Aiden, and Karen, then slipped it into her wallet. Singing along to Aiden's gravelly voice on Night Wind, she combed the tangles out of her freshly washed long hair, and braided it, knowing the auditorium would be warm. The rock ballad Emily crooned from the CD while Jeni applied a light amount of makeup.

You should have asked for another ticket, to invite Karen along. You'd have more fun that way. Not true. Besides, I may have to use the IOU as payment for another picture or CD.

Jeni held up two sets of earrings, trying to decide which looked better. She settled for the simple silver hoops, then ejected the CD from the drive and slipped it into its case.

Enduring the bumper-to-bumper traffic a mile from her destination gave her a chance to calm the butterflies in her stomach. Thirty minutes later, she parked her compact car in its assigned slot near the baseball diamond and joined the crowd making their way to the auditorium.

"I don't know why they didn't hold this at the football stadium," grumbled one attendee. "Surely the football team isn't practicing tonight."

"No, but they do have a game in the morning," reminded his companion. "God forbid the stadium be filled with garbage before the game."

Jeni clutched her purse tight and soon found the Will Call window. She gave her name and showed her drivers license before being issued a ticket. Jeni sucked in her breath.

"Is this right? Surely this seat is already taken." I'm in the third row?

"There are always some seats the band reserves for families or radio show winners. Next!" The woman dismissed her and called for the next person in line.

Jeni clutched her precious ticket and made her way into the building, following the map and signs. She stopped for a hot dog and a soda before finding her seat, and watched the crowd take their seats. Soon the lights dimmed and the warm up act began. Jeni found herself caught up in the mixture of rock and country music and made mental note to get one of their CDs. A brief intermission followed, and then the lights dimmed again and the opening notes of one of Aiden's signature songs began. Jeni leapt to her feet with the others as the stage lights pooled spots on first the keyboards, then guitars, drums, and then Aiden, dressed in black jeans and a loose red shirt. He worked the front rows, and during a ballad, even sat down on the edge of the stage while screaming fans reached for his knees.

Nearly two hours later, Greg appeared at Jeni's side, during an instrumental solo, and motioned for her to follow him.

"But I'm going to miss the last song," Jeni yelled into his ear.

"No you won't; I'm taking you backstage." Greg led her past security personnel and into the wings of the stage. He leaned close to her. "Sing me a few bars of Night Wind."

Jeni frowned. "Why?"

"Just do it, please."

Jeni sighed, concentrated, then sang the chorus. "How was that?"

Greg looked surprised. "Not bad. Okay, here comes Aiden."

Jeni looked up as Aiden appeared, downed an entire bottle of water, then poured a second over his head. "Hi, Jen. I've got that surprise for you." He looked at Greg. "Well?"

Greg nodded, and Aiden's smile grew larger. "Great. We'll hook her up with microphone number four." He drank more of the water, and as the crowd chanted his name, took her hand. "Ready?" He led her out onto the stage and picked up his guitar.

The crowd cheered. "Ten years ago, I stopped in your town with little more than my guitar on my back, and a few cheap demo CDs. Jen here helped out this poor musician when his Jeep broke down, so tonight I've invited her to sing with me. Her favorite song is one of my early ones, so this is for you." He strummed the opening chords and leaned closer to her. "Don't be shy; grab that microphone there and just pretend you're in the shower." He went into the opening lines. Jeni felt her brain lock with panic when she heard the screams and cheers, then felt Aiden's breath on her cheek during a musical pause. She looked into his steady eyes and saw him encourage her with a smile. Taking a deep breath, she added her voice to his, and by the end of the first verse, Jeni felt her confidence pick up. Aiden looked into her eyes as he sang. The stage faded away; she concentrated on his vibrant blue eyes and sang to him. When the last note died away, the roar of the crowd jolted her back to reality. Aiden put his arm around her and kissed her temple. Her knees buckled and a stagehand brought her a stool.

"Sit down, darlin', and enjoy the rest of the encore." Aiden touched her cheek, then turned back to the crowd as Sam played the opening chords to another song.

After the show, Jeni found herself in Aiden's dressing room, being offered everything from candy bars to hamburgers in a warming pan. The band, famished from performing, gobbled food, drank rivers of liquid, and rehashed the show. Aiden led Jeni to a couch, then disappeared into the adjoining room, reappearing in faded jeans and a black T-shirt. He loaded two plates and, after handing her one, sat beside her and joined the conversation.

"What did you think?" He sprinkled salt and pepper on his french fries and took a bite.

"I think you need to warn the people you drag up on stage. You're lucky I was listening to your first CD in the car." Jeni felt her stomach rumble and bit into her hamburger.

"I knew you could handle it. I don't do that very often, but I was prepared to sing it just for you anyway, even if you didn't join in." He chased his fries with a bottle of soda.

"I thought rock-n-roll stars were all drugs and sex backstage." Jeni popped a chunk of mango in her mouth.

Sam laughed. Aiden threw a pillow at him. "I don't allow drugs backstage. As to the sex, well, there's always someone offering, but that doesn't mean I take them up on it. That's more up Ned's alley."

After Aiden finished eating, he stood and held out his hand to Jeni. "Do you have a smart phone?" Jeni pulled it from her pocket and handed it to him. "Gary, take one of us in front of the door." They posed as the drummer snapped their picture, then Aiden handed back her phone, opened the door, and escorted her outside. "I'll catch up with you boys later."

Jeni held tight to his hand as the sound of whistles and cat-calls followed them. Aiden led her to the rear of the stage, then leaned against the expensive looking travel trailer.

"You know you have the distinction of being my first official fan." He let go of her hand and smoothed a stray lock of hair from her face.

"I may be your first official fan, but that doesn't mean I'm your usual groupie." Jeni forced calmness into her voice.

Aiden threw back his head and laughed. "I wasn't implying that you were, darlin'. Let me see that picture."

Jeni reached into her purse and produced the dog-eared photo, along with the yellowed scrap of paper. "I'd say this qualified as showing me a good time. I've never been up on stage with anyone famous, or even backstage."

Aiden shook his head. "You keep it. This is not what I call 'showing you a good time', so we'll table it for another day, okay?" He studied the picture. "Wow, look how young I am."

"I was only fourteen, and you don't have the stress lines in your forehead."

"If you tell me my hair is gray, I'm gettin' on that bus right now."

Jeni laughed. "Hardly. I think I had just gotten the braces removed from my teeth. See, Karen still has hers."

He handed back the photo. "Where's the CD?" He produced a Sharpie and scrawled a note on the back of the cover. "Don't read that until you get home tonight. Where's your car?"

Jeni told him, and together they walked toward the baseball diamond. "Greg would have my ass if he knew I was out here without security, but nearly everyone's gone."

"And they would hardly expect to see you with someone like me." Jeni shivered as a light breeze blew.

Aiden put his arm around her again, offering warmth. "What do you mean, 'someone like you'?"

Jeni mentally smacked herself. "I mean, I'm no supermodel or actress. I've seen you at award shows with beautiful girls."

Aiden snorted. "Greg hired them to be with me, so people wouldn't think I was gay. I'm thirty-five years old, and just because I haven't found the one, the media jumps to conclusions."

They reached Jeni's car and she unlocked it. She leaned against the doorframe and looked up at him. "Thanks again for tonight. I don't read the gossip magazines, but the celebrity TV shows always have good things to say about you, though."

"I partied in my younger days, and got it out of my system. Now I spend my days writing, performing, or in the studio." Aiden yawned. "Sorry, darlin'. Some idiot bellhop snuck into my room and caused a problem which interrupted my sleep." He grinned. "And yes, I'll still come back to your hotel next time I'm in town."

"When will that be?" Jeni raised her eyebrow. "In another ten years?"

"Oh, god, no. I plan to be back as soon as this tour's over. You're the first person I've met who isn't on the total fan wagon over me and the boys." His face grew serious. "If I wasn't so damn tired, I'd take you to breakfast and get to know you a little more, but you have a long day tomorrow, and I have to be in St. Louis tomorrow night. Can we stay in touch until my tour is up in six months?"

Jeni's mind whirled. "You--you want to get to know me better? I'm nobody."

"Honey, 'nobody' wouldn't have kept an unknown rock star's photo or crappy first CD that no record label would touch. The only reason they're playing some of them now is because the first three albums went double-platinum. You've believed in me from the start, haven't you?"

"I just knew I liked what I heard." Jeni's throat went dry.

"That means the world to me." Aiden stepped closer and slanted his lips over hers.

* * *

Aiden felt his gut explode. Ahh, this felt right. For the first time in a long time, he actually felt like he wanted to keep on kissing a girl. Jeni's body felt stiff at first, but she soon relaxed her grip on his biceps, and felt her arms slide around his neck. He ended the kiss and stepped back, enjoying the look of bliss on her face. She opened her eyes and smiled, then blushed bright pink.

"That was nice." She averted her eyes and stuffed the CD in her purse.

"So, can I have your number? Email address? Last name?" He teased.

"Name, rank, and serial number?" She laughed, breaking the tension. "Do you even carry a cell phone?"

"Yes, I do." He pulled it out of his hip pocket and brought up the contacts screen. She rattled off her phone number, then pulled out her own phone and put his private number into hers. "Lassiter. My name's Jennifer Lassiter."

"Well, Jennifer Lassiter, I'll text you tomorrow. In six months, I want to take you out for a nice meal and hear you talk about yourself, since all we did tonight was talk about me." He yawned again. "Sorry, hon. I just thought of something. You are going to fire that bellhop, right?"

Jeni nodded. "Lee did that as he was being carted off to jail. You don't last long in hospitality if you steal from your guests." She opened the car and stepped in. "Can I give you a lift back to your bus? Don't want you getting mobbed or anything."

Aiden nodded and went around to the passenger side. "Thank you."

Molly Daniels

THE SHADOW IN ROOM 313
Floyd Simeon Root

Gypsy realized too late as she shut the door, she had left her dust pan inside the room. Frustrated, she keyed the door open and retrieved it. Her anxiety level rocketed as she realized she was getting even further behind on her work load. I can't afford to get fired again, especially so close to the last time. To make matters worse, she had forgotten her Xanax pills. Pushing her cart on to room 313, Gypsy engaged in an angry internal dialog with her mother as she opened the door and entered. *How dare you treat your daughter the way you did me? What kind of person are you? And how could you leave me like that?* Tears formed in her eyes as she cursed her mother silently. She felt guilty having such thoughts toward a recently deceased person. Her name was the only good thing her mother had left her. Her mother had named her after herself, a full blooded gypsy woman. Gypsy did not even know who her father was.

When her anxiety increased so drastically, Gypsy sometimes became totally disengaged with her immediate environment, sucked into her own internal torment. In such a state she would not even have noticed if two Blue Jays were fighting right under her nose. That was the way she lost her last job, and the one before that. Not paying attention, they said. Out in La-La land, they said. She was startled back to reality as she noticed two feet protruding over the edge of the room's queen-sized bed. The feet appeared feminine and petite. The person was laying across the foot of the bed with the covers drawn over her. Gypsy was fearful she would get chewed out for bursting in on a sleeping customer. Her manager would not be happy with that, no, especially not twice in one day. The first reaction of a rational person would have been to quickly and quietly retreat, close the door, and hope for the best. But Gypsy didn't always react in the most rational manner.

She gazed at the blanket-covered form for signs of movement, tilting her head to focus her vision. The person did not stir. Gypsy was intrigued with how quietly she was laying. She stepped softly toward the far side of the bed, watching closely to see if the covers would rise and fall with breathing. The lady's hair draped over the edge of the bed, and one hand was exposed from beneath the covers. The form seemed awfully quiet. *Is she dead?* Gypsy wondered.

Gypsy slowly reached down to touch her hand, softly and tenderly, so as not to wake her. The hand was cold.

"She's dead," she whispered to no one in particular, and raised the fingers of one hand to her lips.

"Now, isn't that a kick in the butt?" She heard a voice from across the bed toward the door.

Gypsy's eyes widened, and her heart jumped as she recognized the danger. Her access route was blocked. She was sure the voice had come between her and the door. But she saw no one there. Perhaps the voice was coming just outside the door. Then, she saw a faint shadow on the wall. She whirled her head to see if the shadow was formed by a person standing behind her. No one there, either. Her gaze again swept the room looking for something more than the shadow that was still there.

"I said, now isn't that a kick in the butt? Kind of seems like you should say something." The voice seemed mildly perturbed.

"Who...who are you?" Her voice quivered. "And what do you want?"

"I am The Shadow."

"What are you talking about? Are you crazy? Shadows can't talk."

"If shadows can't talk, then I guess you are the crazy one. After all, you are the person who's talking with one."

"I'm not crazy. I don't know what's going on here, but I am actually talking to you and we're having a conversation, so I'm not crazy."

"Say, that's a pretty good deduction. I guess you can't be crazy if you figured that out."

"Stop it! I'm not crazy, so there. So, who are you then, and what do you want?" She tried to sound fearless, but her heart was a trip hammer.

"First, let me close this door. We don't want nosy people dropping in on our little party." The Shadow moved toward the door, and it swung shut.

"Okay, let's start over again. I am The Shadow. I used to be on radio."

"Wh...what do you mean?" Gypsy was so nervous she could hardly speak.

"What I mean is I used to be on the radio. That shouldn't be so hard to understand. I had my own program. I was pretty popular, too. But you wouldn't know anything about that. It was before your time."

"Oh, yeah, well, I've heard of that program, The Shadow. So there."

"Really, now? You've heard of The Shadow? How did you know about me? That was way before your time."

"I bought a CD, at Cracker Barrel, the Oldies but Goodies section. They have all kinds of old radio programs."

"I am impressed." He began to laugh.

"That's it, the diabolical laugh. Yes, I remember now. You were an invincible detective, or super hero, or something like that, and you had that diabolical laugh. 'The Shadow knows….ha, ha, ha, ha.' It was kind of like that."

"Very good. You do a nice imitation of me. I'm flattered."

Gypsy's head was swimming. She rubbed her fingers slowly over her temples.

"What seems to be the problem?" asked the Shadow.

"I have a headache. My day wasn't going very well anyway, and now this."

"I am so sorry. Take that clean glass on the table behind you and fill it with water."

She hesitated.

"Go on. Pick up the glass, and fill it with water.

This time she did as she was told.

"Now, open the desk drawer. Inside you will find a packet of powder. Tear it open, pour the contents in the glass, and set it on the table at the foot of the bed."

She obeyed. "Am I supposed to drink it?"

"No. No. Don't do that. We should be having a visitor just about any time now."

Now Gypsy was really alarmed. "What should we do, then, about the body, I mean? I'll probably get fired. What about the police? The way my day is going, I'll probably get charged with murder." She looked around frantically for a rag. "I better get rid of my finger prints."

"No, don't do that. A maid is expected to leave finger prints when you clean a room. It would look suspicious if there were none. Besides, I have a plan. The police don't have to know, and neither does your manager."

"What about the visitor? What should I do? I know. I won't let her in, that's what."

"Actually, she has a key. She will let herself in."

"She has a key? Oh my God. I'm going to hold the door. She's not coming in.

"How's that going to help? She'll just go get the manager. You'll still have a problem."

"So, what do you suggest I do?"

"Let her come in."

"Let her come in? I'm supposed to just let her walk in and find a body? Are you crazy?"

"You need to trust me on this. Let's assume I know more about this situation than you do. Let's assume I am more capable than you are."

Gypsy laughed nervously. "Just let her walk in? Okay, what am I supposed to say, like 'whoops, we have a body here?' "

"Don't worry about it. I'll control the whole thing."

They heard the rattle of a key being inserted and twisted in the lock, and the door slowly opened. The head of an attractive lady, perhaps in her late twenties, peeked in. She saw first Gypsy, and then the body lying on the bed.

"What happened to Irene?" Her voice seemed flat and rather matter of fact.

"She's dead," said Gypsy. "Come on in and we'll talk about it."

"Of course." The lady eased through the narrowly opened door, closed it behind her, and spoke softly to herself, "Harold is definitely not going to like this."

"Harold already knows."

Gypsy was surprised with her own comment, having no idea why she would say such a thing. "Come on in and we'll talk about it."

"You are the hotel maid, then?"

"Give the lady a prize. She knows a maid when she sees one."

"Are you involved in this some way?"

"I suppose you could say that."

"Why should I believe you?" asked the lady.

"It was Harold's idea. He thought I would be an asset."

"Oh, really? Harold thought it would be a good idea. Interesting."

The lady looked Gypsy over, and then began to pace

back and forth, rubbing her hands over her head and eyes. "You'll have to excuse me. I have a rather intense headache."

"I'm sorry about that," said Gypsy. "I had one myself. I fixed something to get rid of it. Looks like you need it more than I do. You can have it if you wish." She motioned to the glass on top of the table.

"What is it?"

"It's something new, works really well on headaches. My doctor highly recommends it. Can't get it without a prescription, though." She nodded her head toward the glass.

The lady walked to the table, picked up the glass, and drank it down. Gypsy had a feeling of satisfaction which she could not explain. The lady turned and once more began pacing slowly back and forth. "Okay, we need to have a plan. I'll call Harold. Can you secure the room for a while, make sure no one enters?"

"I can do that."

The lady whipped out a phone, dialed, and waited. "Is Harold there? No, it's too early. Listen, we have a problem, big problem. How soon can you get hold of him? It is. Tell him we have a situation in room 313. Tell him to get his butt over here as soon as possible. How long…? No. Good. Thanks."

She flipped her phone shut and stared at Gypsy. "Okay, it'll take him about twenty minutes to get here. Getting rid of the body without drawing anybody's attention is going to be a problem, but it can be done." She interrupted her conversation to steady herself by gripping the table.

"What's wrong?" asked Gypsy.

"I don't know. The headache left, but I feel a little unsteady. I'm getting dizzy. What did you say was in that drink?'

"I didn't. It was something my doctor ordered. I don't remember the medical name." Gypsy wondered at the ease with which she answered the questions. It was almost as if someone else was providing the answers.

"I can hardly stand up. I'm afraid I'm going to pass out," said the lady. She feared a concussion, or messing up her hair, if she fell to the floor. In her ebbing of consciousness, the woman leaned forward, falling across the bed, close to the headboard, as far away from the body as possible. She twitched a few times before relaxing.

Gypsy stared in disbelief, watching for movement in her chest. There was none. She felt for a pulse, first at her wrist and then her neck. Again, nothing. "Oh, my God! Now look what you've done."

"What seems to be the problem?" asked The Shadow, innocently.

"What do you mean, what's the problem? Now I have two dead bodies. This is going from bad to worse."

"Just relax. I have it all under control."

"Relax? Are you crazy? How can you say you have it under control? We have two dead bodies here. What is there about disaster you don't understand?" She rubbed her temples again.

"You still have that headache?"

"Yes! It's getting worse, thanks to you."

"There's headache medication in the desk. It's in a bottle, a green bottle. You need to take two pills. It will relieve your headache. And then I will explain how we're going to fix everything. Trust me, it will all work out fine."

Gypsy had no inclination to trust The Shadow for anything, not the pills, not his promise of everything working out fine. Still, her headache was getting worse. It seemed like she was getting one of her migraine headaches. The headaches didn't come often, but they were unbearable when they did.

"Go on. Take the pills. They will get rid of your head ache." He sounded compassionate.

"We can't just leave them here! We have to do something!"

"You're histrionic. Just like a woman."

"What am I going to do with the bodies? That's like a humongous problem. You don't seem to be concerned. I need some help here."

"You could always haul them out on your cleaning cart."

"That's ridiculous. People can see them."

"You could do them one at a time, make two trips."

"Don't be stupid. They won't fit. You know that. Stop messing with me!" She rubbed her temples again.

"You're getting intense again. Is your headache still bothering you?"

"Yes! It's getting worse."

"You better take the medicine in the green bottle."

Gypsy said nothing, her head bowed, her eyes closed, as she continued to rub her temples.

"Go on. Take them. You will be glad you did. You really don't have much choice. Your headache will be getting worse. You will have to take them sooner or later. The sooner you take them, the sooner you will feel better."

She knew he was right. In resignation, she filled a clean glass with water and retrieved two pills. Swallowing one at a time, she leaned her head back as she gulped water with each pill. She drank most of the water and set the glass on the desk. Gypsy could feel the effects of the pills almost immediately. The headache did seem to be leaving. She felt much more relaxed. Her fear was greatly reduced. She walked around the end of the bed where their feet were and viewed the bodies. The women lay, one on each end of the bed, like they had been neatly arranged. They looked so peaceful. Gypsy even envied them a bit. She wondered if she should make a break for the door. Maybe The Shadow would do nothing to stop her. What could he do? He was only a shadow.

Gypsy noticed that she was starting to feel light-headed. The room was spinning around her. Her legs began to feel rubbery. She wasn't sure she could remain standing. She didn't want to fall to the floor, so she leaned forward and fell onto the bed in perfect alignment between the two bodies. She really didn't want to be lying between two dead bodies, but it didn't seem to bother her. She thought that strange. Normally, the thought of lying between two dead bodies would have terrified her. She felt remarkably peaceful.

Gypsy's thoughts began to drift, dream-like, toward her mother. She felt remorseful. *Mother, I see you. No use trying to hide from me. It won't work. Besides, I want to tell you something. I forgive you. I love you too. I really do. So, come on over here so I can give you a great big hug. I really, really do love you.*

In her deepening fog of sleep, she heard The Shadow say softly, "This is all working out very nicely."

That would be the last thing she would remember.

Floyd Simeon Root

LIZZY GARVIN REMEMBERS BRICK BRAUVELT
J. Travis Grundon

On the morning of October 7, 2011, Brick Brauvelt was found dead in his Florida home by his son Brandon. An autopsy revealed that Brick died as a result of acute heart failure due to underlying atherosclerotic cardiovascular disease. He was 58 years old.

Two days before being found dead in his Florida home, Brick had signed a deal with a major cable network for a weekly reality show. The show was designed to profile the life of a major media icon and his struggle to make a living on his name in the independent wrestling circuit.

Brick Brauvelt was never inducted into the Wrestling Hall of Fame. It didn't matter if you liked him, loved him, or hated him, to the people who knew him, he was a legend.

I remember watching wrestling with my dad. We both got excited every time Brick came out. He was the coolest, but I think my dad only rooted for him because people always said that dad looked like Brick.

It's embarrassing to admit now, but I remember having a life-size poster of The Brickster in my bedroom.

Because my dad and Brick looked so much alike, I never developed a crush on Brick. I always used to think of my dad every time I saw Brick. Brick took on more of a hero's role in my life. He was the reason I wanted to become a pro wrestler.

I thought I wanted to be the Brick Brauvelt of lady's wrestling.

Being a Brick Brauvelt stopped being cool after he got fired from every major wrestling promotion in America. He developed a reputation as someone who was hard to work with, and racked up a bunch of wellness policy violations. After a while, he became a joke.

The first time I worked a show with Brick was at a pretty big indie card in Mexico, just after he was released from his big contract.

I didn't have the guts to go up and talk to him. I was happy just standing backstage with him, listening to his stories. Brick was bitter about being let go as a main event guy on television and Pay Per View, but he still had great stories, and he pulled no punches.

I didn't start to get the impression that he was a prick until he started being rude to the ring crew and the Lucha Libre stars on the card. I don't even know why such a narrow-minded person would agree to wrestle in Mexico. It was embarrassing how racist he was.

"I don't know what the hell these guys are sayin'," he said, "Why can't they learn to speak American?"

My heart broke a little. I wanted to point out that Americans speak English, not American, but I still had some respect for Brick in those days. I was also afraid to be kicked off of the card for disrespecting a legend.

He would never get a second chance to make a first impression with me. I still respected Brick as a wrestler. I gave him the benefit of the doubt because of his recent circumstances, but I had lost interest in him as a fan, and I wasn't sure I liked him as a person. Not that he cared.

I didn't see him again for another two years, when we were both working a series of indie shows in Indiana and Illinois.

Brick had fallen pretty far since the last time I had seen him. He looked like shit. It was hard not to feel sorry for him, wrestling in high school gyms in front of 15 to 20 people, for two thousand dollars a pop.

He hadn't been taking very good care of himself. He'd developed a limp and an unsightly beer belly. He might have even been on some kind of drugs, but I wouldn't have been able to tell what he was on. I wasn't into the drug thing. I only smoked pot with the boys from time to time.

The first night of the tour was pretty mellow. Brick didn't do anything too outrageous. We all worked our matches, and headed back to the hotel for the night. Some people went out for food, and hit the local bars, but most of the talent came back to the hotel room I was sharing with my opponent for the tour, Randy Randy.

I was still a casual Brick fan, but Randy was obsessed. She made it clear that she wanted to sleep with him. She also made it clear that I was to keep my hands off of him, something I was happy to oblige.

Randy had invited Brick back to our room to get high with her and one of the refs, whom we affectionately referred to as Pot-Head Jon. It would have been cool if it had just been the four of us, but when word got around that Brick was hanging out in our room, most of the boys filed in to hang out, too.

The more the Brickster smoked, the more he talked, and the more people ate it up, the mouthier he got.

He went on for hours. "I'll tell all you guys something right now, after you've wrestled in Madison Square Garden, in front of sell-out crowds, these high school gyms and bingo halls don't cut it. It's like having sex with a beautiful woman every night. Now, I'm lucky to hook up with some 16 year-old tramp who doesn't know a blow job from a rim job."

As if he hadn't made a horrible enough first impression so long ago, now there was no way to deny the kind of person he actually was.

The worst was when he came into the female locker room while I was getting dressed. I was completely naked, so when he came in I covered myself with a towel and waited for him to leave. But he didn't leave. He said that he was looking for Randy Randy, but he just stood there and stared at me.

I eventually snatched up my gear and darted into the restroom to get ready.

When I came back out to work out my match with Randy, all I saw was Brick's big white ass bouncing up and down on the floor, with Randy sprawled out beneath him. I'm not sure if I was more pissed at him or Randy. It wasn't only gross as all get out, but it was also rude as hell that Randy would fuck him in the locker room we had to share.

I wasn't interested in watching anyone have sex, so I took my stuff up to the curtain to watch the show, instead. When I got up to the curtain, everyone was looking for Brick. He was supposed to already be on his way to the ring, for a run-in save.

The idea was that he was going to save the company's champion, Joey Frankenstein, setting up a big tag team match for the main event. It didn't work out that way, because nobody could find Brick. The only thing they could do was just keep beating Joey down, until somebody found Brick.

Rudy asked me if I had seen him, and I told him the truth. I said that he was he was bangin' Randy in the girls' locker room

Brick's signature music was already playing, so Rudy asked me to go get him. I agreed. But to this day I wish I would have refused, because when I got back to the locker room, Brick was pulling up his trunks, and Randy was lying on the floor like a glazed doughnut. This was a sight I didn't need.

I told Brick that he was supposed to be in the ring, but

he didn't care. He told me: "When you're the champ, people'll wait!"

His attitude made me sick. After all, these people did pay to see him, but he was too busy bangin' a glorified ring rat to go out there and do what he was getting paid to do. It also pissed me off, because he was getting paid three times as much as me.

I couldn't stop thinking that he was a creepy piece of crap, but it only got worse when he opened his mouth. "You know Randy, next time we do this, we should toss your little friend in the mix." He suggested, looking at me. "You'd like that, wouldn't ya, baby!"

At that point, if looks could kill, the look Randy gave me would have stopped my heart. I didn't want anything to do with Brick. As he walked out of the room, he slapped me on the ass. He laughed, but Randy didn't find it funny at all.

Randy scoffed, wiped herself off, and got dressed, keeping her eyes on me the whole time. "Brick's mine, bitch! You'd better keep your damn hands off him."

That night when Randy and I met in the ring, I took her to task by wrestling the stiffest match I've ever worked. I loved every minute of it, but Randy ran to the promoter. The card schedule was changed, and I wrestled my friend, Chardonnay, for the rest of the tour.

Randy got to be Brick's valet.

During the remainder of the tour, Chardonnay was switched to my room. I'm not sure if Randy ended up staying in Brick's room, and I didn't care. I was just happy to have a no-bullshit roommate.

I thought it was the end of the Brick drama, but things got even more weird when we got to our hotel the next night.

After we checked in, Chardonnay and I decided to change and have a few drinks in the hotel bar with the boys, but when we were getting changed, she stopped suddenly and covered herself. She was staring intently at the window, specifically at the slight part in the curtains.

"Girl, I think there's somebody at the window," she said, as she scurried into the bathroom.

I hadn't even noticed the curtains were partially open. I wasn't completely undressed. I was still in my underwear, picking out what I was going to wear, when I turned to see that she was right. It wasn't a big deal until I walked over to close the curtains, and I saw something move outside.

I whipped the curtains open. I couldn't believe it, Brick Brauvelt was standing outside the window. He was fumbling with his belt, and when the curtain flew open, he ducked behind the other side of the bushes. He was sneaking behind the bushes, and stayed low. A few rooms down, he popped up and jogged into the hotel lobby. He'd obviously been masturbating at the window, watching while Char and I were getting undressed.

Without even grabbing my robe, I stormed out of the room. I marched down to the hotel lobby, but Brick wasn't there. The promoter, Vance Idol, told me that he hadn't seen Brick all night, but Idol had a reputation for lying to his talent.

Of course, Idol just laughed when I told him what had happened. "Don't worry about it," he said. "I'm sure you'd like to think Brick Brauvelt was jacking off to you, but I don't really think that's the case."

Several others of the wrestlers standing in the lobby found the whole thing pretty funny. I don't think any of them took it seriously, except Randy Randy. She wasn't in the lobby to hear my story, but she somehow caught wind of the incident.

Her reaction was the most idiotic thing in the history of pro wrestling. She actually hunted me down. I knew that she was looking for me, but, to my disappointment, she wasn't looking for a fight.

When she found me, she made it point to tell me:

"There is no way a superstar like Brick Brauvelt would ever masturbate to you, when he was with me all night!"

I let her have her opinion.

Chardonnay and I stopped working for Vance Idol after that tour, and we both agreed to never work with Brick Brauvelt or Randy Randy again. The only good that came from meeting Brick was learning how disappointing the wrestling business can be. He taught me that it's never a good idea to meet your heroes.

My dad wasn't surprised when I told him what had happened. He started hinting around for me to quit, and stopped watching wrestling. He only watched it when I was home from the road, but even that stopped when they started crossing unbelievable lines. I can't even watch this crap they call wrestling now. I swear, one time I turned on Monday Night Wrestling, and saw The Giant jumping on his dad's casket while The Boss dragged it through a cemetery with a car.

My dad looked at me and said, "What in the hell am I watching here?"

After that, I didn't watch wrestling on TV for years. I was too busy watching footage of my opponent's old tapes, and training my ass off. I felt that the big companies had lost sight of what wrestling was all about. It became "sports entertainment."

The last thing I ever saw on TV was a guy handcuffed to a ring post, while his opponent hooked jumper cables up to his gonads. I haven't watched it since. I haven't even stepped foot in a wrestling ring. It wasn't worth it.

I'm perfectly happy managing my hotel and teaching yoga in my spare time.

I try not to think about wrestling or Brick Brauvelt. I was shocked to hear that he had passed away, but I honestly can't say that I'm sad about it. A bastard in life is a bastard in death.

J. Travis Grundon

AN EXCERPT FROM:
MAN AND MONSTER
James M. Bowers

Sloppy

The scene was too perfect, that should have clued me into the fact that it wasn't real. She lay beside me with her head on my chest while her fingers traced random patterns on my stomach. The smell of her filled my nose. I loved every bit of it, from the faint fruity shampoo aroma in her dark hair, to the spice of her sweat from our recent exertions. She lifted her head and our eyes locked in the faint white light that seemed to come from all around.

"You have to go." Her voice was so sweet to hear. I wanted her to talk for hours.

"I just got here." When had I got there?

"They are coming." She reached a hand up and placed a finger across my lips. I kissed it and talked past it.

"They don't scare me."

"I'll be here when you get back." The room started fading. I felt my eyes close and fought the feeling of falling away from her. When my eyes once again opened, the sight was much less pleasant. I stared up from the vinyl chair, where I had apparently passed out, and stared at the yellowed acoustic tiles lit garishly from the neon vacancy sign right outside. I took a deep breath. That was a mistake. The memory of smells from the dream were quickly replaced with the smell of years of cigarette smoke, stained sheets, and disappointments. I fought the urge to cough, and tried not to breathe back in through my nose. I heard the sound then. Heavy footsteps, coming toward the door.

Over the years, I've learned to put a lot of faith in deadbolts. In the rare occasions I've had with people trying to kick my door down, a dead bolt tends to make their job a bit tougher. Sadly, the cheap hotel I was in didn't understand the value of deadbolts, or even real wooden doors. I heard the footsteps speed up in their approach, and turned to see the cheap door fly apart in a somewhat impressive shower of splinters and some kind of white powder. Adrenaline flowed through my body from the shock and everything slowed down to a crawl. I saw the plastic hotel cup on the carpet in front of me, a bit of low end scotch drying and staining the horrible carpet. The table beside me still held half a bottle of the foul drink, its cap tightly screwed on. The muscle-bound door-kicker entered the room, and I felt a smile spread across my face as I went into motion. He was focused on the bed and held a mean looking sawed off double barrel at about waist height. My right hand wrapped around the neck of the bottle, and I flung myself out of the chair and twisted, aiming for the back of his head by way of his face. The bottle was surprisingly thick for the cheap stuff, and I thought I could hear bone crush a bit from the impact. He dropped in an awkward pile, and I scrambled for the shotgun. I hoped it was loaded.

"What the?" I pointed the gun in the general direction of the doorway and pulled the trigger. The sound of it going off in the small room hit me like a hammer to the chest. The shape in the doorway slumped forward, and the hall outside resembled some impromptu abstract art. I had no idea if there were more of them out in the hall as the only thing I could hear was my nearly destroyed eardrums. I padded over to the nightstand by the bed and retrieved my little .25 pistol from the drawer. Sloppy of me to have passed out in the chair. Though I had been lucky, I couldn't afford such sloppiness. I crouched low in the doorway to the bathroom and tried to will my ears to heal up so I could have an idea what was going on. The pistol went into my pocket. I checked the shotgun. At least I still had a round left. The adrenaline rush made me have to fight to stay still. I forced my heart rate down, and my hearing recovered after a few moments. A few more moments of waiting, and still no sound or movement. I moved to the big man's body and fished for his wallet one-handed. I found his phone and his wallet, and put them both in my other pocket. I really didn't feel like being covered in blood, so I skipped searching the other body. I did a quick peek out in the hall and saw nothing. I gathered up my jacket from the back of the chair and dropped the shotgun, before stepping carefully over the body in the doorway. I found a fire alarm halfway down the hall and pulled it. The alarm blared and those few that had slept through the shotgun blast peeked out of their doors. I put on a friendly smile and walked toward the back exit.

The Start of A Long Night

"What a fucking mess."

"I really wish you wouldn't smoke in the crime scene, Greg."

"This guy doesn't care anymore." Greg flicked ashes on the carpet in the hall.

"No. I suppose he doesn't, but the lab personnel feel a bit differently."

"Fine." He pinched the cigarette out and put the remainder in the pack. "This doesn't look much like a mob hit to me."

"Agreed. The mob tends to not to leave behind such messes. At least, not in my town."

Greg stepped over the body in the door and into the

room. He walked over to the larger body on the floor and bent down just as a flashbulb went off.

"What the fuck?" He swatted in the direction of the photographer with a thick, fingered hand. "Thanks, now I can't fucking see." Greg rubbed his eyes. "Karl, will you get this little shit out of here before I can see what he looks like?" I walked up and stood beside him.

"Give us a moment please." The photographer was a young one. Fresh out of school, I would bet, his face a bit green and wearing an expression of fear. "Go get some air. We'll be out of your way in a moment."

"Sure, detective. Sorry." He stepped over the body in the doorway and out of the room.

Greg opened his eyes again and blinked rapidly a few times.

"It appears as though his skull was caved in." I crouched down beside the big body on the carpet and looked at what was left of the guy's face. Whatever had hit him had caved in the front and right side of his skull. The impact was horrendous.

"With what? Fuck, Karl, I can't see a fucking thing. Fucking amateur photographers." I clicked on my flashlight and looked around.

"Apparently with this." I pointed out a half empty scotch bottle.

"Don't those usually break?"

"You watch too many movies, Greg." I stood and walked to the doorway. I waved for the photographer to come back in.

"So. We have two bodies, two different murder weapons, and the killer left us both of them?" Greg was still rubbing his eyes as he walked over to me.

"It seems that way."

"Why didn't they just leave a confession and stay to get picked up, as well?"

"Nothing is that easy, Greg." I stepped over the body

and out of the room. "Come on. Let's grab a bite and wait for the lab boys to finish."

"I saw a greasy spoon across the street. I wonder if they have pancakes this late?"

"We can only hope." I waited for Greg to hop over the body, and turned down the hall. I let Greg lead as I went over the scene in my head. Nothing here made any sense. What kind of killer takes out two of the mob's hard-boys, but leaves so much evidence behind. "I hope they also have good coffee." It looked to be the start of a long day.

Coffee and Lowriders

The diner was a real shithole, but the coffee was at least drinkable. Luckily, my standards for coffee were pretty low. The place was mostly empty of customers and I had my choice of tables. I picked a booth near the back exit, my back to the wall. I took the stolen phone out of my pocket and removed the battery. I'd have to strip its contents later, but it would be sloppy to leave it on, and I had been sloppy enough lately. I sipped the black coffee and debated on ordering food. I pulled the stolen wallet out and flipped through it. It was a cheap, black tri-fold, with a picture of a crucifix printed cheaply on it. Ripping apart the Velcro seemed loud in the empty diner. A library card was the only ID, now, that was a new one. Danil Karantirov had apparently been a reader, at least until just recently when I caved in his skull with a cheap scotch bottle. I sighed and dug further into the wallet. He had a couple hundred in cash, and I pulled that out and stuck it in my pocket. I put the wallet back in my pocket, and flipped through the menu, finding nothing that sounded appealing. I wouldn't get anything done sitting around. I was about to motion for the waitress to bring me a check for the coffee when I saw two policemen walk in. The boys in blue had been in and out of here for a while getting coffee, but these men wore suits.

The man in front was older and wore a cheap suit that quite possibly could have come from a thrift store. He looked to be in his early forties, and was short and stocky. He seemed to not have shaved in a few days, and he wore a battered brown fedora. He took off the hat to reveal very close cut brown hair. He held the door open, with nicotine stained fingers, for the man behind him. The second man walked through with a thankful nod. He towered over his partner. At more than six feet, according to the height chart on the door frame. His suit was high end and very well tailored. He was well groomed with a clean shaven head. His face held hard, slightly angular features. I couldn't tell any more detail from across the room. He seemed deep in thought but still scanned the room for a few seconds before entering. I avoided eye contact. They took a table by the door, and I stood up to leave. I reached in my pocket and pulled out a fifty. I tossed it on the table and walked out the back, hoping it wasn't alarmed. Luckily, it wasn't. I walked away from the diner and turned the first corner I reached. I didn't like the look of that detective. What was a man in that kind of job doing wearing a suit that expensive? I would have to do some digging, too many things about tonight didn't add up. I had only walked a few blocks from the diner and was debating calling for a cab, when a large car rolled up beside me.

"What the fuck do you think you're out doing in our neighborhood?"

"Yeah, motherfucker."

I glanced over to see two neighborhood punks eyeballing me. Shitty neighborhood all around. I put on a friendly smile and walked to their car. This was apparently unexpected.

"Say, either of you boys have a smoke I could bum? I seem to be out." I patted my suit jacket pocket and put on a sad expression. Their confusion lasted long enough for me to close the distance to the driver side door. I reached through the open window and smashed the driver's head hard against the steering wheel. His nose smashed flat and blood flowed almost instantly. He was, of course, not wearing a seatbelt, and I pulled him through the open window. I tossed him aside and opened the car door as he rolled to a stop, still too stunned to even scream. I slid into the driver seat and stared over at his friend.

"You should get out now." I wore the smile again and that seemed to do the trick. It took him three tries to find the door handle, then he was out and running. I adjusted the mirror and pulled away. This would do at least till I could get uptown.

Pancakes

"Hey! They do have pancakes!" Greg seemed genuinely excited. I frowned at the back table where the only other customer had recently been sitting.

"Don't you find it odd that he left just as soon as we came in?" I stood up and walked toward the back table.

"Not really. No one likes cops these days." Greg went back to the menu.

"Do they usually leave a fifty dollar tip for coffee?"

"Do what now?" The waitress walked toward me with the coffee pot. She reached for the tip. I stopped her just before she would have snatched it up.

"Here." I opened my wallet and took out a hundred, barely looking at it. I passed it to her. "I'll take the fifty." I pulled a latex glove from my pocket and used it to pick up the bill. "Greg, do you have a baggie left in your coat pocket?"

"Sure, just a sec." Greg pulled out a few evidence bags and tossed them on the table. He seemed unconcerned. I retrieved the bags, then slipped the bill and glove into one bag, and using a second glove, put the coffee cup into another. Greg looked up from over top of the menu. "You gonna order any food?"

"Order me a coffee and a burger, please." I slipped the bags into my jacket pocket, then placed the jacket on the back of the chair across from Greg. "I'm going to go wash up." I walked to the bathroom as the waitress came over to take Greg's order.

I came back to the table as the waitress was pouring the coffee. There was a commotion at the door as a couple of teenagers came in. One was supporting the other, who had blood staining all down the front of his shirt and pants. He was very pale.

"Help! I can't get him to stop bleeding." I grabbed the napkin dispenser from the table and rushed over. Greg sipped his coffee.

"What happened?" I helped the injured boy to sit at the closest table, pulling napkins from the dispenser. I pushed them over the boy's nose and had his friend hold them there.

"Greg, call for the EMT's please."

"We were just cruising around, ya know. Enjoying the night. When some crazy Mamón in a suit came at us, waving a gun! He broke Miguel's nose and made me get out of the car. Then he just drove off in it!"

"Just keep holding that tightly. Help will be along soon." I pulled out my phone, flipped it open and hit the speed dial. "I need an APB out on a, just a sec." I looked to the boys. "What does your car look like?"

"It's a red 1970 Chevy Impala. We just got it painted and tuned up."

"You got that? Thank you." I turned back to the kids. "What did this guy look like?"

"He was shorter than you. White, I guess, with black hair. He was wearing a light grey suit. Had a really creepy smile."

I looked up and around along the ceiling, but didn't see any cameras. "Any security cameras in this place?" I focused on the waitress.

"Nah. Too expensive." She chewed her gum loudly and walked back toward the kitchen, seemingly uninterested now that the excitement was over.

Hot Showers and Burglary

The stolen Impala rode rather rough and I wondered what was wrong with it till I saw all the hydraulic controls. I rolled my eyes and focused on driving through the city uptown, while avoiding the highways. I dropped the car off behind a grocery store and walked the next few blocks to a slightly rundown apartment complex. Walking around back, I took the key from above the door frame and let myself into the landlord's apartment. There was a coating of dust on everything. I would have to come back here more often, or hire it out. I shook my head again at my sloppiness of late. The pile of mail at the front door was almost comical. I considered clearing it, then decided to wait till later. I flicked on the lights, and after some argument they came to life. I checked the fridge to find it, thankfully, empty. I grabbed the cordless phone off the wall and dialed the local grocery store. I hoped they still delivered. The phone only rang once.

"Yeah?" A young voice, bored, probably a teen working over the summer.

"Do you guys have coffee pots for sale?"

"Duh." I resisted the urge to just walk over to the store and choke the little shit.

"Well, bring me one, and a few bags of your light roast coffee." I tried to keep the anger out of my voice.

"We don't deliver anymore. We stopped that, like, months ago, man." The phone crushed to pieces in my hand before I even realized that the anger had hit me. I sighed and grabbed the broom and dustpan. I worked on clearing out my head by cleaning the apartment. The mail all went into the trash, save for the personal letters from the other tenants. I would either read those or leave them for whoever took over this place. A few hours later, and the apartment was clean but I was filthy. I turned on the shower. After some protest and a horrible brown-colored water, it was soon running hot and clear. The shower and the ordered apartment cleared my head again. I was even whistling to myself as I opened the wardrobe. The whistle died on my lips. All my clothing was gone. I always made sure to stock all my places with at least a basic suit and exercise clothing. The anger flared as I put back on my sweat stained suit. I checked for the rest of my gear. The small desk was empty of both the laptop and handgun I usually kept there. I checked all the windows till I found where the punks had broken in. I had thought the windows all painted shut, but they had somehow gotten the one by the back door open. Sloppy. I rubbed my palm down my face and walked out of the apartment, leaving the keys on the kitchen table. Fuck it. Let them have it.

There was a bar a few blocks down. A drink sounded like a grand idea.

A Big Fucking Mess

"They found the car." Greg looked up from his phone, across his empty plate to me.

"Where?" I stood, my food lying mostly untouched on my plate. I wasn't usually hungry when on an active case, and forcing myself to eat diner food was always a chore.

"You're not gonna eat that?"

"I don't believe so. You can have it. Now, where is the car?"

"Uptown. Left behind a grocery store. No cameras on the place. Guy could be anywhere by now. They're bringing the car in." Greg snatched up the plate and dug in, ketchup dripping down onto his tie. He didn't seem to notice.

"You're disgusting to watch." I sat back down and waited.

"I know!" Greg smiled, then took another large bite. He made short work of the burger, and I stood and reached for my wallet.

"I got this one." Greg waved a ketchup smeared hand at me. He cleaned his hands with napkins and checked his reflection in the side of the napkin holder. He seemed satisfied till he looked down and saw his tie. "Man. I just bought this!" He tried to clean most of it off with napkins, but it was already too late. He stood and grabbed his wallet. He tossed a couple twenties on the table and nodded his thanks to me as I held the door and we walked out.

We walked back across to the hotel parking lot. Greg drove an old Toyota Tercel from the mid eighties. It always smoked when he started it, and I always had to be careful not to kick food trash out on the ground when I climbed in.

"Your car smells horrible, Greg." I wrinkled my nose and closed the door and rolled the window down.

"You could always clean it, Karl." I lit a cigarette, pulling the foul smoke into my lungs as Greg started the car and pulled out of the lot.

"Why is it that you drove this time?" I blew smoke out the window.

"Cause I would like to live a little longer." Greg looked over at me. "Got one of those for me?" I shrugged and lit another cigarette to pass over.

"Thanks. These things'll kill ya, ya know?" Greg took a long drag and blew the smoke out his window.

"Not very likely." I rubbed at the headache coming on at my temples. "More likely we will end from gunshot wounds."

"You always take the fun out of it." Greg pushed down on the gas and, for once, actually drove above the speed limit toward the precinct.

The precinct was mostly quiet this time of night. Greg went to check what was in the vending machine and I went to the lab to check in evidence.

The lab took up the entire fourth floor and was in stark contrast to the rest of the building. The main, three story police station was first built in 1927 when the city was booming. It boasted authority in its art deco style, but over the years city budgets hadn't allowed for maintenance. Paint peeled from the tops of the halls, and cracked and stained mosaic tile littered the entryway. The lab was added five years ago when I donated fifty million for its construction. It was well built and continued the bold, clean art deco style, but everything above the third floor shined with the brightness of the new. A simple brass plaque was fixed upon the wall beside the doors to the fourth floor.

In Honor of Kendrick and Etta Williams.

I touched the names on the plaque and felt the cold brass as I passed into the lab. The lab had a scent of strong disinfectant to it that was refreshing after the smells of the cheap hotel, diner, and Greg's terrible car.

"Who the fuck would be bothering me at this hour?" The voice filtered over from behind a bank of equipment.

"Sorry to be a bother. Should I come back later?"

"Karl? Is that you?" The tone turned sweet. The grating squeak of the wheels of a desk chair, and a young face peeked from around the row of machines. "Karl!" The sweet tone turned to one of excitement, and I had to brace myself as the lab tech threw herself at me. I smiled and tried not to laugh.

"You're getting way too old for that." I set her back down.

"Don't you mean that you're getting too old for that?" She giggled a bit.

"Ha. Ha." I gave her a serious face but couldn't maintain it. I broke into a wide smile a few seconds later. "Mia, are you busy?"

"Not too busy for you." She held out her hands like a young child waiting for a gift. She even closed her eyes. "Gimmie!"

Mia Reynolds was the youngest forensic scientist in the state. She graduated from High School at thirteen, and had her first degree at fifteen. A lawyer friend, whose child had shared a class with Mia, had found out about the clever girl and told me about her in passing. I did some more research and found that she was extremely gifted in the sciences, with a passion for forensics. I had funded her education anonymously afterward. She found out who had paid for her school after two months, and had tracked me down. She had threatened to brain herself on the pavement if I didn't tell her why I would do such a thing. Her explanation for such an act being that she would not be in debt to me, or anyone else. I never could handle her very well. I informed her that I needed a lab tech very badly, just as soon as she could get there. We came to an agreement and now, at the age of seventeen, she ran the lab.

"It's not your birthday." I gave her the serious look again, held it this time.

She opened one eye and glared at me. "No. That was last Tuesday. You missed it."

"You've always been a bad liar. You should give it up. I know that it's next Thursday, and you won't get any early presents." I stuck my tongue out at her. She mirrored the expression.

"So what do you have for me? Is this about those Russian guys at the hotel?" Her eyes got wide.

"How do you know they were Russian?"

"Oh. You just got in, right? Just a sec." She ran back behind the equipment, her long braids bouncing behind her, and returned with a file folder. "Here."

"You know you aren't supposed to have these." I gave her what I hoped was my disappointed glare.

"I know." She shrugged. "Now what do you have for

me?"

I sighed and reached into my jacket pocket. I handed her the evidence bags. "I need prints off these, and DNA from the cup if you can get it." She took the bags greedily and walked carefully back behind the wall of tech. "I'll come back later." She waved a hand at me from above a monitor. I shook my head and walked out. I opened the file and glanced through it on my way down the stairs. The victims were both naturalized citizens from Russia, though just recently. Danil Karantirov had spent ten years in Владимирский централ (Vladimir Central Prison) for assault upon a member of the military. Semyon Spravtsev had spent five years for human trafficking in Atwater. He had been released last month on a technicality, having served only two years. Evidence had been lost or improperly filed, and was caught on appeal. I reached the second floor, and was just about to walk through the doors and find my desk when my phone went off. I closed the folder and flipped open the phone carefully, pressing a button on the front after looking at it for a few seconds.

"Hello?"

"Detective? This is Sarah Daniels. Could you come down here when you get a chance?"

"On my way." I closed the phone and walked on down the stairs and through the steel doors into the basement. It was cool down here and smelled strongly of chemicals, with an undertone of death and decay. I pushed through the double doors and into the morgue.

"That was fast." Sarah Daniels was rather short for a coroner at only five feet. She wore her auburn hair pulled up tight into a ponytail. Her lab coat was buttoned crookedly as if she had been in a hurry.

"I was on my way down from the Lab."

"Oh." Sarah's gaze focused somewhere past me. I cleared my throat.

"So. What did you want to see me about?"

"These guys have some very interesting tattoos." She walked over and opened two doors, pulling the drawers out. She folded the sheet back away from the head of the body on the left. "This guy has a spider in a web that covers the entire back of his head." She moved to the other body and folded the sheet back to his waist. "This guy has a rather large bull, here on his chest." I looked at both tattoos closely.

"Interesting. Have you photographed these?"

"Of course. I just thought you would want to see them in person."

"Thank you." I straightened. "Is there anything else you would like me to see?"

"No." Sarah blushed slightly. "That's it."

"Thank you. Call me if you find anything else." I turned and walked quickly out.

Greg was at his desk when I finally made it back up to the second floor. He had his laptop open and was cursing at it while trying to type something with his thick fingers. He had an open bag of pretzels beside him and I reached over and took one from the bag. It was a bit stale and I didn't bother stealing another. I leaned back in my chair and took in the room. It was mostly quiet. Late night and midweek was usually like that. Crime always seemed to flare up on the weekends. Greg and I were the only detectives at work. Office interns buzzed about, filing one thing or another around the edges of the long room. My eyes wandered over toward the large carving in the wall. It was a simple, yet elegant, rendition of Lady Justice, her blindfold pulled tight over her eyes. The scales in one outstretched hand, the sword held upright in the other. The Lady had been carved out of black marble in a stark contrast to the white tile of the rest of the wall. Her sword and scales were forged by hand from bronze that shone with a well-aged patina. My eyes drifted down from the Lady to the beat up desk in front of me. Few of the desks matched out of the ten left in the main room. The desk in the main office was original to the building, but none of the rest were. Some were even sitting upon books to make their heights match the ones next to them. I debated just replacing them all, but there was something comforting about the mismatch. A bit of chaos, inside the stark order of the art deco.

"Hey!" Greg's fingers snapped at me. "You gonna daydream all fucking night or are we going to work?"

"Sorry." I shook my head. "What's going on?"

"Apparently there was a bit of a problem at a bar near where they found your boy's car. You wanna go check it out?"

"Nothing else to do yet. We may as well." I stood. "We're going to need more coffee, though." I glared at Greg. "This time, I drive."

We made it across town in less than ten minutes without running any stops, and only slightly cheating on the speed limit. Traffic was rather light this late at night, which gave me some good opportunities to rush a bit. I needed to hit the racetrack soon. The urge to really cut loose was getting hard to ignore lately. The car was a dream to drive, the feeling of all that barely contained power in my hands was thrilling. I did slide a bit around a few curves, but slowed back down when I glanced over at Greg's face. His pallor matched the young photographer's from earlier. At the bar, we had to park more than a block away, for all the police cruisers and ambulances.

"Five meat wagons for a bar fight?" Greg lit a cigarette and leaned against a nearby light pole, his color slowly coming back. "Seems a bit excessive, don't you think?"

"I suppose we should go find that out. Can you walk?"

"Yeah. I'm fine. I just wish you would drive like a normal crazy person."

"I took it easy. You should come to the track with me sometime."

"No, thanks. If I wanted to be sick I could go ride a

roller coaster."

I smiled but he missed it. We pushed through the crowd of emergency personal and overly curious citizens. We made it through to the bar, and the inside looked like a war zone. The floor was covered in bits of broken glass that crunched underfoot. Several tables were turned over, and even a few of the stout chairs were broken. The bartender stood behind the bar as if rooted to the spot. He looked to be in his mid forties. Blood was splattered across his face. A streak of blood ran through his hair where it looked like he had pushed it back off of his face with a blood covered hand. His eyes were open wide but unfocused. He was talking softly to an officer across the bar from him. I left the officer to his task and walked slowly around, trying not to disturb anything more than all the EMT's already had. Here and there were splatters or pools of blood. The light glinted on something, and after closer examination with my flashlight, it turned out to be a golden tooth, bloody and broken off at the root. Greg tapped me on the shoulder.

"Up there." He pointed and I looked up. There was a jackalope mounted firmly to the wall, a little over halfway to the ceiling. Only short broken stubs remained of the horns that had been screwed to the rabbit skull. The whole thing was covered with blood and viscera. "What the fuck?" I looked back to Greg, he looked a bit spooked.

"Indeed. Let's find out." I sought out the officer in command. He appeared to have finished with the bartender and was on his way out, staring down at his notebook. I fell into step beside him and asked the obvious.

"What happened here?" He seemed to jump a bit as if he hadn't heard me crunch up beside him.

"My apologies, Detective. I didn't see you come in." The officer seemed a bit out of it. I motioned for us to walk outside. The fresh air seemed to do him some good. His gaze locked onto the lights of the nearest ambulance. "Have you ever seen something like that?"

"No. I can't say that I have. How many people were hurt?"

"Sixteen. Five fatalities. A few more of them may not make it through the night." He shook his head as if to clear it.

"How many Perps?"

"One." He looked eyes with me. "They all have the same story. Or similar enough. It was just one guy. Some fucking monster." He shook his head again. "I've gotta go write this up. See you back at the station?"

"Of course. What's the description of the Perp?"

"Early 30's, Caucasian, male, black hair, wearing a grey suit. Though, by now, that suit is probably stained a bit red." He chuckled at that. He fought it down. "You'll have my report within the hour, Sir." He nodded to me and walked to the nearest cruiser.

"Who the fuck is this guy?" Greg's tone held disgust tinged with just a bit of awe.

"Or what." I took out the pack and lit two cigarettes, passing one to Greg. We stood in silence until the last ambulance pulled away.

To Be Continued...

CLOWNS
Jean DeSanto Campbell

She was tired. She threw her suitcase on the bed and turned on the lamp. Then changed her mind and decided to open the curtains. She was in a room at the back of the hotel, so she thought there would only be a view of the desert sands she'd glimpsed as she drove into the parking lot. She was wrong. For some reason, there were clowns in the parking lot.

Lena's day had started miles away, in Chicago. She had finished early what she needed to do at work, run home and grabbed her suitcase, and dashed to the airport. Well, as much as one could dash to O'Hare. Luckily, she could take the train and not have to navigate the stupid Dan Ryan Expressway. Another advantage of living near the Loop. She needed to remember to use that next time she was arguing with her mother about the dangers of downtown living.

Of course the plane to Vegas was full. There was a group of college football players celebrating the season. Loud and inebriated, they partied the whole way. She sighed with relief when the plane reached Vegas and she could get her rental car and head out of town. She didn't gamble, and the city held no lure for her beyond a gateway to the place she was headed. Death Valley.

She had traveled through once or twice on her way to LA from Vegas just for fun. That was years ago. The area always intrigued her, with the heat and the sand and the word Death in its name. What could possibly live there, she had wondered. Then she passed through on the desolate rocky highway, and saw the resorts that made their stand in the desert. She read about the deep history, had been enchanted by the stories of miners and adventurers, and she knew that one day she would go and stay for awhile. When she got the bonus at the end of October, for working hard and not making a fuss when they promoted Charlie instead of her, she knew exactly what she wanted to use it on. She needed to have some time alone, some time and space without family. She put in for extra days of vacation around Thanksgiving. She called her mother and told her she wouldn't be home for the holiday. She had a "work trip" she couldn't get out of. There was squawking, but not as much as if her mother knew Lena was choosing not to attend a family gathering. At some point Lena would have the courage to tell her, but she wasn't there yet.

Trying to book a hotel this late was iffy, she knew. She'd tried the four places in the National Park, hoping. There was a cancellation at the final place she called. She knew it was a chance, trying to book a holiday weekend so close to the holiday. But, as if she was being called to the desert, there was a room at the Devil's Fire Resort. All the accommodations had names based on fire and brimstone. It was a titillation for the timid, a calling for adventurous risk takers, those willing to brave the heat and barrenness of the lowest place on earth.

Lena told everyone at work that she was spending Thanksgiving at her sister's in Denver. Todd in accounting tried to make a date for sometime during the weekend because his family was in Colorado Springs, but she blew him off with a story about how her sister needed her to help with the baby since it was her sister's first time to host the family. Part of the story was true, it had just happened five years ago when the baby was born. She hoped she wasn't storing up bad karma lying to everyone, but she just needed this one thing that was hers, and only hers. Nobody asking annoying questions about why she would go there, and why was she abandoning her family. She wasn't abandoning her family. She was family to herself, wasn't she? She deserved not to have to spend every single free moment with the extended family, just because she wasn't married anymore.

Lena sighed, remembering, and stared out the window of the room. Which should have had a view of the sand dunes across the desert, but instead blocking her view was a bunch of clowns. Literally, ten people in clown makeup and costume were sitting under umbrellas, drinking from water bottles while a cameraman fiddled with a camera. It was almost sunset, so Lena supposed it was some sort of surreal photo shoot for a fashion magazine. They were only a few hours from Vegas in one direction, and a few hours from LA the other, so it could be anything, really. Cirque du Soliel, Vogue, some ridiculous art installation. Oh, well, it would make things interesting if the performers were staying for the whole weekend. Maybe they would have some interesting stories to tell. She eyed her laptop, which had the beginnings of her novel. The reason (or so she told herself) that she wanted to be alone in the isolation of the desert.

The novel she had been working on since college. Through the marriage to Brad, who had sucked all the creativity out of her with his neediness, through the marketing job that paid the bills and kept her busy. Ten years of saying, soon I will have the down time to work on this, but all the while getting pulled this way and that by family, by a cheating husband whom she hadn't really cared had cheated, since he only cared about himself in bed anyway. Finally shucking him off like an ear of Delta sweet corn, and finally able to breathe, now. She lay on the bed for a rest. At least there was no cell service and no internet. On the WiFi level, Death Valley was in no man's land. Only land lines in the form of a couple of pay phones, and the phones and reservation computers in the front office could connect. So no one would be bothering her. She smiled and closed her eyes. That, at least, was heavenly.

Lena woke with a start. She must have been more exhausted than she thought. She looked out the window of the room. It was dark. Her stomach rumbled. She could feel her blood sugar dipping. Blech. She had better eat, or there would be problems there. She sighed as she looked in the mirror. Her hair was sticking up from napping on the bed. One of the troubles with short hair. It tended to stick up and be hard to smooth down. She rummaged in her bag for her comb.

Changing from her traveling clothes into jeans and a polo shirt made her feel better. She knew there were two options for food, a restaurant and a bar. She glanced at the clock. It was 9:30 p.m. already. Okay, that narrowed her choice to the bar. She hoped that the food was better than bar food usually was. As she went out the door, she glanced at the laptop again. What a cliché I am. Woman with novel. Will travel.

The desert air was dry on her face as she walked from her room around to the front of the hotel and towards the common areas, but not particularly hot for November. Nowhere near the 116 degrees it would be in July. She felt the warmth in her bones, enjoying it. So different from the chilly November she had left behind in Chicago, and the frigid temperatures that would accompany the snow in Denver.

She pushed open the door to the bar. Inside, the noise, and the chill of the conditioned air were a pleasant change from her solitude. Maybe I just need the company of people who don't know me, she thought, people without an expectation for me to have a particular role to play.

A bar full of strangers reflected in the bright lights off

the mirror behind the vintage counter, which ran the whole length of the bar. Most of the bar stools and tables were full with chattering people who seemed to know each other well. They were probably all part of the photo shoot, done for the evening. Lena headed for an empty place at the end of the bar. She smiled at the man in the next seat over.

"May I see a food menu?" she asked the bartender. She looked at the drink menu written in chalk behind the bartender's head. Some intriguing drinks were listed, with names like Death Trap Ale and Fizzy Pitchfork, and a few IPA's, with some others on tap that she recognized. The bartender handed her a menu.

"What'll you have to drink?"

"Surprise me with something local," she said, pointing to the board. The bartender grinned.

"Do you like dark or light?"

"Darker, the better."

"Okay, how 'bout I give you the Devil's Knot? It's a fine dark, wheat lager. If you like meat on your beer, you'll like it just fine."

The bartender turned away to grab a beer from the bin full of ice in front of the mirrored wall, and then placed the bottle and an empty frosted glass in front of Lena. Her neighbor looked on in approval, and held up his own bottle. It was the same beer. Lena grinned. She poured the beer slowly into the glass, letting the head settle before she took a drink. It was good. She smiled in appreciation at the bartender and opened the menu.

"Where are you from?" Her neighbor seemed to want to talk. That was fine with Lena. She was ready for some small talk, without any strings attached, at least for awhile, anyway. She ordered a buffalo burger and onion rings from the bartender, and turned to answer the question.

"Chicago. How about you?" She looked in his eyes as she answered. They were brown, and she liked brown eyes. They were warmer than blue eyes. Brown eyes always seemed nicer, even when they weren't attached to a nice person. Like her ex-husband. She sighed. Nope. Don't go there. She took another drink of the very good ale.

"We're from LA." He motioned to a group at a table by the front of the bar. "We're here doing a photo shoot. Clowns in the desert. It's for a perfume ad." He laughed. "We'll be here for a few days. The photographer always wants to take shots in every sort of light; she says that the more angles we get, the better. Since I get paid by the hour, that's fine by me. I'm avoiding the whole group of them right now, because I'm tired of them already." He made a wry expression with his eyebrows. Lena laughed.

His hands were tan and big, with long fingers, the nails nicely trimmed and buffed. She couldn't help noticing as he took a drink of his beer. She had a thing for hands. She couldn't stand short, pudgy hands on a man. Or long fingernails. Long fingernails on a man made her skin crawl, and reminded her of Dracula. You have so many hang-ups. But no compromise on the nails, she told herself.

Lena looked at him more closely. He was quite beautiful. The brown eyes were surrounded by thick black lashes, and his brown hair was rich and curled slightly, giving him a faintly Italian-Adonis look. His accent was pure valley girl, though. She smiled.

"My name's Lena. What's yours, pretty boy?" She couldn't help it. He was pretty. She took another drink.

He looked at her.

"Pretty boy, really? I'm a person, not an object!" He couldn't keep a straight face. That was good. He had a sense of humor. Nice.

"My name is Nick. Nice to meet you, tomboy. Cool haircut." He pointed to her pixie cut. "And I should know cute, I'm a male model." He fluttered those eyelashes at her. She snorted.

"Yeah, yeah, a male model dressed like a clown." Although, he wasn't dressed like a clown at the moment. He was very attractively dressed in jeans and a white button-down shirt.

"A clown working on his Ph.D. in mechanical engineering. I'm just modeling to put myself through school, really. And stripping on the side. Grad school is expensive."

"Really? Stripping and modeling. When do you have time to study and work on your thesis?" Lena rolled her eyes.

"I'm not really a stripper. Or a model." Nick made it sound like it was a confession. "The photographer for the shoot is my sister, and I'm helping her out. Some of her real models are idiots, and I keep them in line. Plus, I get to dress like a clown. Another fantasy to cross off my list."

Nick cleared his throat. "Nah, Linden doesn't really need my help. She can handle her crew. I'm just here for fun. And the money. I really do like getting paid." He motioned for another beer from the bartender. Lena finished hers. Her burger and onion rings appeared. The smell made her mouth water. She looked at Nick.

"I'm going to apologize in advance. I'm a sloppy, enthusiastic eater, unlike the models you have been hanging out with. So you may be disgusted. But, hey, that's life in the real world."

He laughed. She picked up the burger and took a big bite. It tasted as good as it smelled. The onion rings were homemade. They were nice and hot, and the breading on them was crunchy, just the way she liked it. Hunger won out over being polite, and she briefly forgot about Nick as she ate. She could hear him talking to the person on his other side. When her food was finished, she suddenly was tired again. She paid for her meal and her drinks, and touched Nick's arm as she got down from her stool. He turned to her.

"It was a pleasure to meet you, pretty-boy model clown engineer. I think I covered all the bases there. I'll see you around." She shook his hand, gravely, trying not to smile. He shook his head.

"You are a funny woman. Don't you know it is impolite to dismiss a man so early in the evening? We're quite fragile. But, if you must go, I shall recover." He saluted her mockingly as she headed for the door.

"What a clown you are!" She laughed at him as she left the cool and the brightness of the bar.

Outside, the night desert air had cooled, and the sky was full of stars. She tried to pick out the constellations she could remember from when she was a child. In Chicago, so much light pollution obscured the stars that she had forgotten how many stars actually filled the sky. Nights in the city were full of her coworkers and friends, spent at happy hours and shows or concerts. Not a lot of contemplation allowed. That was something she missed. She took a deep breath and let it out. She needed this long weekend for herself. And maybe a bit of clowning around would be allowed. She laughed. I'm so clever. She headed back to her room.

THE GREEN LADY OF WEST BADEN
Jennifer Christian Sebring

My auburn hair doesn't shine with its coppery glimmer any more, neither do my eyes flash with their emerald spark. My cotton skirts with the voluminous petticoats underneath no longer make their traditional 'swish' as I walk by. These days, I am merely a shadow in the corner of your eye, or a passing whisper. I, my friends, am a ghost. Here, they call me 'The Green Lady'. How did I become this specter wandering the halls here? I think it is best that I start from the very beginning.

Before I was "The Green Lady", I was known as Cora Mae Shaw, and I lived in Evansville, Indiana. Being the youngest daughter of an investment banker in Evansville, there were few marriage prospects for me in 1904. It was hoped that I would continue my education, and in doing so secure employment for myself, now that I had completed high school. I had already accepted a position at a local newspaper as a typist, and the job was to begin in roughly two weeks' time. I planned on going to the Women's College roughly 200 miles away in Terre Haute. My Aunt Mabel had written a letter congratulating me on my completion of high school, and as a graduation gift, invited me to join her for a week at the West Baden Hotel.

I am very excited to travel by train to the town of West Baden. When I arrive, Aunt Mabel meets me at the train station, and we take a horse-drawn cab over to the hotel. As we crest the hill, the hotel is spread out before us like a castle in a fairytale. I had never seen anything quite like it. Aunt Mabel notices the awestruck look on my face, leans over and whispers, "It's the largest dome in the world. Now, don't gawk child, it's not ladylike."

"I didn't mean to gawk Aunt Mabel, but this place is magnificent!"

"That it is, Cora Dear. I thought you could use a bit of pampering before you join the workforce, and there is no better place around here to get that pampering. The mineral baths here will cure you of anything that ails you," Aunt Mabel says to me, as she looks me over. Her eyes fall upon my faded purple gown, and she exclaims, "Goodness gracious, child! You wore *that* onto the train?" I look down at my dress, and twist the gloves in my hands.

"I didn't want to wear my good clothes on the train because I didn't want to soil them," I reply, looking down and blushing. Aunt Mabel gently lifts up my chin so that I look her in the eye.

"Darling, you remind me of your mother more with every passing day. She was always so practical." I smile and blush in return.

"I do miss her very much," I reply to Aunt Mabel.

"I know you do. Now that we are here, why don't you go to our room and change? We are in room 318. I will be in the atrium, you can find me there," she tells me as she hands me a large skeleton key with '318' engraved on the end.

"Yes, Aunt Mabel," I reply as I take the key from my Aunt's hands, and walk towards the stairs. Climbing three flights of stairs, I reach the third floor. After a few moments of following the bronze number plaques on the wall, I find our room. I place the key into the keyhole and turn it. The lock in the door makes a dull clunk sound and the knob turns, the door swinging open wide. I walk through the open doorway, then close and lock the door behind me. The room is fairly large, with a king-sized bed to one side of the room. A washstand is next to a very ornate vanity.

"What a beautiful room," I whisper to myself as I open up my trunk, which the bellman has placed at the foot of the bed, and I pull out my day dress. It is made of pale blue damask, and has a slight ruffle at the bottom hem. I remove the hatpins holding my hat to my hair, and gently lift the hat off my head. Quickly, I change dresses, and replace my hat and gloves. Before I leave the room, I look myself over in the mirror, and dab a bit of rose balm on my lips and cheeks. I walk towards the door and unlock it. The heavy clunk of the tumblers in the door tells me that I can turn the knob.

I open the door to a quiet hallway. Quickly, I turn around and lock the door behind me. I gather up my skirts in my left hand, and make my way down the hallway to the stairs. After descending the three flights of stairs, I enter the atrium of the hotel. It is a magnificent sight! The ceiling rises up like the great palaces in Europe which I have seen in books. In the center of the atrium is a splendid fountain. I spot my Aunt Mabel sitting at a table, talking with a young man in a strange military uniform. I approached the table, and the young man stands up and acknowledges my presence. Aunt Mabel looks up and smiles.

"Ahh, you look much better now." She gently gestures towards the young man and says, "Mr. Arthur Evans, may I introduce you to my niece, Miss Cora Shaw?"

"It is a sincere pleasure, Miss Shaw," Mr. Evans replies, his voice thick with a British accent. I blush slightly and smile.

"Mr. Evans was just telling me of his studies out at the Walter Reed Army Hospital, and of his time with the

British Royal Medical Corps. I thought you would enjoy talking with someone close to your own age while you are here, Cora. Please, come and sit with us," Aunt Mabel says, gesturing toward the empty chair. Mr. Evans quickly steps over and helps me sit down, pushing the chair up to the table for me.

"Thank you," I tell him.

"Think nothing of it, my lady," Mr. Evans says as he returns to his own seat across the table.

"So, you are part of the British Army, but you are in America?" I ask, puzzled.

"Yes," Mr. Evans replies. "I am a medical officer with the British Army, and I am studying advanced medical techniques at Walter Reed Army Hospital. One of the Generals out there suggested this resort to me. He thought I could use the sunshine and the fresh air for a few days," says Mr. Evans, smiling. "Say, they are going to have a ball here tonight, would you allow me to escort you?" he asks. I look at my aunt with apprehension. My Aunt nods and smiles.

"I would love to!" I tell him, smiling.

"Splendid. I will meet you at the grand staircase in the lobby around seven o'clock, then?"

"Yes. Thank you."

The pleasure is all mine." Mr. Evans says, smiling. I return the smile and blush slightly.

Mr. Evans then tells us of his adventures during the Second Boer War, and his travels in South Africa. He gracefully omits any gruesome details, but he tells of the beautiful landscape he explored on his time off, and the strange animals he encountered. I sit and listen to him, completely entranced with the way that the light dances in his ice blue eyes. Suddenly, the clock chimes, announcing the hour is five in the evening.

"My Dear, if you wish to attend the ball, I suggest you retire to our room and begin getting ready. I shall be right behind you," my aunt reminds me. I stand up from the table. Mr. Evans also stands, acknowledging my departure. I make the trek up the stairs to our room, and unlock the door with the heavy brass key. Once inside the room, I unlock my trunk again, and pull out my fancy green satin ball gown. I lay it out on the bedspread and smooth out any creases. Walking over to the vanity to unpin my hat, I hear a knock at the door.

"Come in!" I call out and my aunt walks in and spies the gown lying spread out on the bed.

"What a lovely gown! Where did you get it? The beading on the bodice is simply divine!" My aunt cries out as she walks over to the bed and holds up the gown.

"Mother and Father bought this gown for me about two years ago, for my birthday. They thought I should have a nice dress to go to parties and such things," I explain as I finish unpinning my hat. My aunt walks over and helps me out of my dress. I take out all the of the pins in my hair, and let it fall in auburn waves down my back. Aunt Mabel picks up the brush from inside my trunk and begins to brush my hair.

"So, what do you think of him?" Aunt Mabel asks me as she brushes my hair with long strokes.

"I think he is quite handsome and intelligent. But, Aunt Mabel, I hardly think it will lead to anything," I reply, as I turn around to face her.

"Why not?" she asks.

"Because, as soon as this week is over, he will be back across the country at the Army hospital, and eventually go back to England. I will enjoy his company and conversation, but that is as far as it goes. I simply do not want to have my heart broken. Besides, I doubt he hardly feels anything but friendship towards me," I reply, looking down sadly.

"Well, if he asks you to write him, will you?"

"Of course I will."

"Good," Aunt Mabel replies as she helps me into my

gown. The emerald green satin is cool against my skin. Aunt Mabel laces up the back of the bodice for me. I smooth out the wrinkles on the front of the bodice, and look into the mirror. Aunt Mabel gathers up my hair and piles it into an elaborate bouffant, securing it with pins. Then she places two combs studded with green rhinestones matching my dress into my hair. She steps out from behind me and looks at my reflection in the mirror. "You look absolutely radiant, my dear, so grown up." I smile and blush.

"Thank you, Aunt Mabel," I reply. Aunt Mabel walks over to her trunk and opens it.

From inside, she withdraws a small box wrapped with a bow.

"This is for you. I saw it in a store window the other day, and I thought it matched your eyes almost perfectly," she says as she hands me the box. I remove the ribbon and open it. Inside the box is a small, beautiful, pear-shaped emerald on a delicate chain. My eyes light up.

"Oh, my! Thank you so much Aunt Mabel! I have never seen anything like it!"

"Neither had I. I have never seen an emerald quite that shade of green before, and I thought it would look beautiful on you. It appears that I chose correctly, because, not only does it match your eyes, but your gown as well. Here, allow me to put it on." I turn around and allow her to place the necklace around my neck. It hangs just at my breastbone.

The coldness of the metal surprises me, but it quickly warms against my skin. I look at the clock on the vanity and cry out.

"Oh, goodness! It's almost six, already? I need to change my stockings and shoes! Aunt Mabel, are you not going to change?" I ask.

"Oh, of course, dear. But you finish getting ready and meet your escort, and I will be along shortly. I don't want you to be late meeting Mr. Evans."

"Thank you, Aunt Mabel!" I reply as I quickly change from my black woolen stockings and boots, to my white openwork stockings and a pair of black satin slippers. I walk back over to the vanity mirror one last time to ensure everything is in its proper place; no underpinnings peeking out from anywhere, and no wrinkles in my gown. I pull on my long white kid gloves as I turn to face my aunt. I ask her, "Do I look presentable?"

"My dear, you look gorgeous," she replies, smiling broadly.

"Thank you, Aunt Mabel." I tell her, smiling in return.

"Now, go. It would be very rude to keep your escort waiting," Aunt Mabel says as she quickly and gently ushers me out of the room. I make my way to the stairwell and descend the three flights of stairs, and at the very bottom I gaze across the expansive lobby. I see a striking male figure who is standing at the right banister of the grand staircase. I cross the lobby and walk up to the man at the stairs.

"Good evening, Mr. Evans," I tell him. He smiles and extends the crook of his arm to me.

"Hello, Miss Shaw. May I say you look absolutely exquisite tonight!" As he looks into my eyes, I see my own reflection shining in his bright blue eyes. I notice a strange symbol on a pin which is pinned to his left lapel. He notices me looking at the pin and smiles. He tells me, "That is the Square and Compass. A symbol of a secret society I belong to, but I didn't tell you that." He winks at me, and I blush. We cross the lobby area into the lushly decorated ballroom. The orchestra is playing a slow waltz as we enter. Candles glow all around us. Mr. Evans takes my hand and leads me to the dance floor. He places his hand at my waist and we begin to waltz.

"Thank you for inviting me to the ball, Mr. Evans."

"It was my pleasure, my lady," Mr. Evans replies gently. "Please, call me Art. Calling me Mr. Evans makes me sound so old!"

"Ok, Art," I say, giggling slightly. "You may call me Cora." I smile as he spins me around the dance floor. A few moments later, the waltz ends, and the dancers stop and applaud the musicians. Art extends his arm to me, and we walk to one end of the ballroom, toward several well-dressed men.

"Cora, I want to introduce you to several of my friends," he whispers to me. I nod in reply. Art escorts me over to the group of gentlemen.

"Lieutenant Evans, who is this angel you have on your arm?" asks a gentleman with a large, white mustache.

"Captain Hubbard, Sir, this is Miss Cora Shaw," Art replies, smiling broadly.

"She is quite lovely. How did you meet her?" asks another gentleman who standing next to Captain Hubbard.

"She was introduced to me by her aunt earlier today, when we met after their arrival, General Adams, Sir," Art replies to him.

"How wonderful!" General Adams exclaims. He turns and looks at me. He asks me, "How are you liking this beautiful place?"

"Well, sir, I have never seen anything like it in my entire life! It reminds me of the pictures of European palaces I have seen in books," I say as I smile broadly.

"This place is quite splendid indeed, my dear," says General Adams. A moment later, the orchestra starts again, playing a lively polka. Captain Hubbard looks towards the orchestra and says to me, "Ah, pity, I was going to ask the young lady to dance, but I feel this is a dance best done by a younger man." Art smiles at Captain Hubbard, and leads me out again to the dance floor. I look up at him and say, "But, Art, I don't know how to do this dance." Art smiles, leans closer to me, and says softly, "It is just like the last one, only faster. Hold on!"I smile as he whirls me around the dance floor. Everything is a blur around us. Swirls of color from all of the ladies' gowns fly past my eyes. Art's cologne wafts into my nose and I am quite taken with its woody scent. A few moments later, the song ends and the room erupts into applause.

"After that dance, I bet you would like some punch," Art says to me as he leads me off the dance floor.

"Why, yes, very much so! Thank you!" I reply as Art releases my arm, giving me a quick bow and walking over to the refreshment table. A few moments later, Art returns with two glasses of a pinkish liquid. "I think it is strawberry," Art says to me as he hands me the crystal cup. I take a sip, and the flavor of strawberry is almost overwhelming.

"It's delicious!" I cry over the din of the crowd. Suddenly, the room begins to spin. I look over at Art, who has a deeply concerned look upon his face. I look up at him and ask, "Art, did that punch have any alcohol in it?"

"Heavens, no! Cora, are you not well? Here, let's get you to a chair," he says to me gently, as he guides me to a chair along the wall. The pounding inside my head is utterly deafening. Suddenly, everything turns blindingly white, then pitch black. I can hear but not see Art as he calls out my name anxiously, and exclaims for his superior officers. They gently place me on the ballroom floor. I can hear orders to clear the area and give me air, and for someone to fetch some brandy. I feel someone rub the pungent liquid on my wrists, and it burns as it is rubbed on my gums.

A few minutes later, I can feel myself being lifted and carried. I am unsure of the destination until I hear the sound of the tumbler as a key turns in the lock. I can faintly hear Aunt Mabel's voice filling with panic, "What is wrong with her? Why will she not wake?" she asks.

"I am not certain, Mrs. Davenport, but all signs are pointing to an aneurysm." says General Adams.

"What does that mean? How does this happen?" Aunt Mabel's voice is becoming frantic.

"Sadly, it means most likely that a blood vessel inside her

brain has ruptured. It could happen to anyone, at any time, unfortunately," Art replies. I can feel a hand lift up each eyelid as they look into my eyes. All I can see are blurry shapes.

"One pupil is larger than the other, and both are bloodshot, sir," Art tells someone off to his left.

"This is grave, grave indeed," replies Captain Hubbard. I hear Aunt Mabel cry out, and then a loud thump. Art yells out for the brandy yet again, and a few moments later, I hear Aunt Mabel mumbling and apologizing. Suddenly, everything becomes muffled, and then silent. I could feel myself rising up away from where I had been lying. My vision is returned to me, and I can see myself lying on the bed, surrounded by people. I see my body shake violently, and then lie still. Art leans over and places two fingers on my neck, and shakes his head sadly.

"She's gone," he says.

Aunt Mabel wails, and faints again. I watch from above as they quickly revive her and Art leads her gently out of the room.

A few moments later, a tall gentleman and a slightly shorter younger man, both dressed in black, walk into the room and up to the bed where my lifeless form lies, and they cover me with a blanket laying by my feet. I finally realize what has happened. I have died.

"NO!" I scream. I shake my head violently and scream, "NO!" again. Then I am floating through the wall into the hallway. Aunt Mabel is slumped down against the wall, weeping. Art sits next to her, attempting to console her.

"Mrs. Davenport -" Art starts to say, but Aunt Mabel cuts him off.

"Please, why did this happen to her? Why her? Why not me?" Aunt Mabel asks aloud, her voice wavering.

"It could happen to anyone, Mrs. Davenport. Even those as healthy as young Cora," Captain Hubbard says to Aunt Mabel.

"What happens now?" asks Aunt Mabel as she looks at the Undertaker.

"Well, Madam," The Undertaker begins, "we prepare the body for viewing by the family. First, though, the young lady's family must be contacted."

"I will fetch the telegraph operator to send the message." Captain Hubbard walks off toward the main lobby of the hotel.

"Madam, we must begin preparing the body due to the weather. Since it is so warm, naturally..." he tapers off, and then resums, "certain processes start to occur."

"Do what you must, but make her look presentable for her father when he arrives." Aunt Mabel buries her face into her hands. Art comforts her, and then reaches to help her to her feet.

"Come, come, Mrs. Davenport, let us get you a cup of tea. No need for us to be present during this unpleasantness," Art tells her as he guides her down the stairs and toward the atrium of the hotel.

Suddenly, I hear an unfamiliar voice call out my name.

"Cora Mae Shaw." I turn around. Before me is a luminous figure. He shines like a thousand stars, and has a pair of silvery wings that gleam.

"Who, or what, are you?" I ask.

"My name is Thanatos. I am merely a guide. I show departed souls the way into the afterlife."

"But what if I don't want to leave yet? My aunt needs me."

"Why would you want to tarry here? Do you not want to go into Paradise?" Thanatos asks. I simply shake my head.

"Because there are people here who need me," I reply to him. He nods, understanding my hesitation to depart, and then says to me, "Very well, I can allow you to tarry on this plane for one hundred of your human years. But it comes with a price. No one can hear you nor see you, and you will be unable to leave this structure until I come back to fetch you."

"All right. I agree to these terms," I tell him, and he vanishes in a flash of brilliant light. It is blinding and all-enveloping, stunning me and rendering me unable to see or hear anything.

By the time my senses return to me, a full day is passed. I look around and everything is draped in black. I make my way into the atrium of the hotel, awkwardly floating through the halls, and sometimes through individuals. I see a line of people by a low table. I see my father, dressed in his best suit and wearing a black arm band of mourning on his left arm. I also see Art among the crowd; he, too, is wearing a black arm band. Aunt Mabel is also here, of course, along with other relatives and many of my school friends. I see Art make it up to the low table. I move in for a closer look. The low table holds my coffin, with my now lifeless form laid inside it, still wearing my green ball gown from the night before. Art leans down towards my face and whispers into my ear.

"I'm sorry I couldn't save you. I would have married you." Art quickly walks away, wiping a tear from his eye. I wail in despair and try to flee the building, to escape my pain. This discovery leaves me utterly heartbroken. He harbored feelings for me and I had no idea! But, just as Thanatos had said, I was unable to leave the walls of the hotel. Out of sheer frustration, I float into the hallway, knocking every portrait off the wall as I pass, using every ounce of energy I could muster.

I wander through the halls in this manner for many years, causing people to do double-takes, questioning themselves as to if they really saw me. For years, I live on in the memory of this place, in hushed whispers as the "Green Lady", a shadowy figure lurking in hallways and doorways, always wearing the same green ball gown I was buried in.

One day, I see the stewards of the hotel line up cots and sedan chairs in a great circle in the atrium. Curious, I move to my favorite observation point, a third floor balcony, and watch as young men in military uniforms are brought in on litters. Many of these young men are covered in bloody bandages. In complete awe of what is unfolding before my eyes, I move down to the ground floor for a better look. Standing in a doorway is a young man in uniform, bearing a grievous wound to his chest. He turns and looks at me as I draw near to him.

"You can see me?" I ask him. He nods and smiles.

"Sure can, Miss." The gentleman says to me.

"Are you in great pain?"

"Well, a few moments ago I was, but not any longer. I don't think I'm going to make it home this time. My name is David. David Ambrose, of Whitechapel, Mississippi."

"Very nice to meet you David, I'm Cora Shaw from Evansville, Indiana. Tell me, Mr. Ambrose, in your travels during the war did you ever meet a British medical officer by the name of Lieutenant Arthur Evans?"

"Do you mean Colonel Evans? Yes, I knew him. He was a very brave man. He died trying to save his men from a mustard gas attack in the Argonne Forest," David replies.

Tears well up in my eyes. Suddenly, a brilliant light shines all around David. He lookes at it and says, "Well, it appears that my carriage has arrived. It was lovely to have met you, Miss Shaw." He then dissolves into the light that surrounded him.

"So, he is in Paradise, hopefully waiting on me," I mutter to myself as I make my way past the front desk, and notice the newspaper sitting in the front lobby. The date reads April 23rd, 1918. "Almost fifteen years have passed since I died. How much longer must I linger here until I can rejoin my mother and Art?" I ask aloud as I drift past a well-dressed gentleman. The sound of my far off voice causes the man to turn around, only to gaze upon empty air. I drift aimlessly throughout the hotel, until I make my way to the very top of the dome, where the painted angels resided.

There I stay for many years, drowning in my sorrow. I come down from my perch every so often, and look around, causing people to become startled at my transparent form.

Now, I watch as the hotel slowly empties, and the plaster recedes from the walls, and here I shall wait until Thanatos comes to collect me, and I can be rejoined with my family and Art.

ABOUT THE AUTHORS

James M. Bowers is a dabbler in many things. His other works can be found at amazon.com. He can be contacted at jaities@gmail.com

Jean DeSanto Campbell writes poetry and short stories while exiled to Southern Indiana. She did go to Death Valley with her youngest daughter but there were no clowns.
You may email her at jeandesanto@gmail.com
She has two blogs:
The Labyrinth Calls at: http://bunnyliebowitz.tumblr.com/
Word Absinthe at:
http://wordabsinthe.wordpress.com/
She was previously published in the anthology *Quixotic: Not Everyday Love Stories* available on Amazon.

Molly Daniels resides in the Midwest with her husband, three children, and various household pets. Her fifth-grade teacher showed this avid reader how to write the stories swirling in her head, successfully unleashing her imagination upon the written word. She is also a devoted chocoholic.
Kenzie Michaels is the 'wild child' of author Molly Daniels. They cohabit nicely inside the brain of a woman in Indiana; mother of three, and 'Aunt Molly' to the entire neighborhood. Molly's husband has learned to watch out when the characters in her head take over, and to not get too upset when the words are flowing and all concept of time is lost.
Books by Molly Daniels:
The Arbor University Tales, Love on the Rocks, Endless Love, Love Finds A Way, Searching For Love, Forbidden Love, Love Weighs In, and Balancing Act.
Available at Secret Cravings Publishing:
www.store.secretcravingspublishing.com

Amazon: www.Amazon.com
Barnes and Noble: www.Barnesandnoble.com
As Kenzie Michaels:
The Anderson Chronicles Trilogy, All She Ever Wanted, Appetite For Desire*, Class Reunion, Teacher's Pet, Off The Clock, Wild At Heart*, The Chosen Series (Sci-Fi Romance)*, Book #1: Heart's Last Chance. Books #2-#5 arriving 2015 and 2016
Available at Freya's Bower Publishing:
www.freyasbower.com
*Available at Secret Cravings Publishing:
www.store.secretcravingspublishing.com

Molly Daniels/Kenzie Michaels' Website:
www.mollydaniels.wordpress.com
I love to connect with readers! My social media links can be found on the Home Page of my website.

J. Travis Grundon is the author of Happy Hour Blues and Mr. Bad Example. He lives in Indiana. You can find him on Twitter @JtravisGrundon

Benjamin Martinson was raised in Vincennes, Indiana. He fell in love with fantasy when he read the King Arthur legends at a young age. He has continued reading ever since. He has always had an active imagination, but he didn't start writing until college. He currently has several books in the work, and his first novel coming out tentatively soon.

N E Riggs is a mathematician and Chicago native now living in Vincennes. There are two series: the epic fantasy series Shadows of an Empire (Book 1: Tomb of the Moon) and the sci-fi action series Only the Inevitable (Book 1: Center of the Universe). NERiggs.com.

Floyd Root I was raised on a farm in oppressive poverty, but I was happy because I didn't know any better. My profession is now in the healthcare field where caring for the infirm is a purpose I cherish. I believe the most glorious human achievement is victory over adversity, the essence of divinity. I believe that life is precious, our past is mysterious, and our future is glorious.

My writings include *Mystic Waters*, *Legend of the Wabash*, *The Legend Prayer*, and *The Benefactor*, a 90,000 word novel which I anticipate will stimulate some interesting conversation. I plan to publish a second novel in the near future. I write with passion, profundity, and polypompocosity.

Contact floyd.root@gmail.com

Jennifer Christian Sebring took to writing as a way to harness her inner insanity. She possesses a Bachelor of Science degree from Indiana State University in English. When she is not creating new worlds inside her head, she can be found knitting, drawing, ghost-hunting, or painting. Jennifer currently lives in Vincennes, Indiana with her husband Chuck, her daughter Lydia, their dog Hailey, and their three cats; Graham, Coco Chanel, and Radar.

Made in the USA
Columbia, SC
14 October 2024

43569522R00076